RAW ICE

PENNY WISE

Fulton Books, Inc.
Meadville, PA

Published by Fulton Books 2020

ISBN 978-1-64654-076-1 (paperback)
ISBN 978-1-64654-077-8 (digital)

Printed in the United States of America

This story is dedicated to my mother, Christine
Wise, and my unborn son, Nehemiah Cassius
Wise. You will go on to do great things.

BOOK 1

CHAPTER 1

LOUD SCREAMS SHATTERED THE QUIET of the dark night and awoke eleven-year-old Aldolphus Jackson. Aldolphus had lived a procession of hardships and nightmares beginning at birth. He was the product of an interracial marriage. His skin complexion was a high yellow, and he possessed the bluest and coldest eyes imaginable. He resented his mixed heritage.

He always relived his first day at Crenshaw Elementary. When his classmates saw that his mother was black and his father was white, they chanted obscenities at him and called him Zebra Head, a name he grew to hate with an intense passion.

Aldolphus played over in his mind the day he walked in from school to find his mother and father stark naked in the living room, seated on the sofa. His mother had a belt tied tightly around her arm, and his father was sticking a large syringe filled with a yellowish substance into her arm. His mother began convulsing slightly, then lay back onto the sofa in a relaxed fashion. Aldolphus walked farther into the room. Sofia's eyes fluttered open and fixed on her son. She jumped to her feet and grabbed her housecoat.

"What in the hell are you doing sneaking around the house?" she snapped while glaring at him.

Aldolphus was a very sensitive child. Tears instantly began forming in his eyes. "I wasn't sneaking around, Mama. I just came in from school. On my way home, I saw Mr. Airstead, and he gave me this," he said, pulling out a fifty-dollar bill.

Sofia walked over and snatched it from the child's hand. "How many times do I have to tell you to stay away from Airstead Gaddafi?" she snapped. "Didn't I tell you not to walk past the ballroom on

Compton Avenue? Didn't I?" she screamed as she slapped him across the face.

He rubbed his cheek to stop the burning. "I didn't, Mama. I swear," he whimpered. "Mr. Airstead was waiting for me outside of the school building."

"Waiting for you?" she questioned.

"That's it," snapped Clevio, getting to his feet and putting on his housecoat. "The next time I find out you were anywhere near Airstead Gaddafi, you're going to be put in foster care, understood?" he said, glaring at Aldolphus.

Aldolphus looked at the tall man's brown eyes and replied, "Yes, Daddy."

Clevio ran his fingers through his blond hair, then turned on his heels and headed toward the kitchen. Sofia knelt before her son. She caressed his small face between her palms and wiped his flushed cheeks with her thumb.

"What did he say to you?" she asked in a soft voice.

Aldolphus looked into her beautiful face, her copper eyes filled with water. He often wondered why his eyes were the color of clear pools while his mother's and father's were both different shades of brown.

"He didn't say anything. He just gave me the money and walked away," he responded in a tiny voice.

Sofia hugged Aldolphus close to her. Tears ran down her face. "I'm only hard on you because I love you. One day you'll under-stand," she whispered. She kissed his lips. "Go to your room, baby." She finished, slapping him gently on his bottom. Aldolphus walked up the steps of the old house and headed down the hall toward his bedroom.

In the quiet of his small room, the child found peace. He was allowed to dream his own dreams and feel his own feelings. Aldolphus walked over and peered out of his window. He always felt so differ-ent from the other children in the projects. His life was lonely and restricted while theirs were open and free.

The only person that showed Aldolphus any sort of affection was a local drug dealer named Airstead Gaddafi. Airstead was a tall Italian man in his late twenties, with blue eyes and thick, curly, black hair. He often spoke in a soft whisper. Airstead was feared and respected throughout the city of Compton. Every Thanksgiving, he'd hand out free turkeys to all the single women in the projects. On one occasion, Airstead had seen Aldolphus on the playground across the street from the projects. After he'd closed his turkey truck down for the day, he gracefully walked over to the child and handed him a turkey.

"Take this home to your mother," he'd said, smiling at Aldolphus.

The child was so happy that he ran all the way home. When Sofia asked him about where he'd gotten it, and he told her he had gotten it from Mr. Airstead, Sofia became inflamed with anger and made Aldolphus throw the turkey into the trash. The small child spent his Thanksgiving Day crying in the darkness of his room with his shadows.

Screams coming from downstairs broke his time of reflection. He swung his legs over the side of his bed and crept down the dark hall. As he reached the top of the stairs, he realized the screams were from his mother, bringing a severe tightness to his little chest.

"Sonny, I'll get your money. I promise!" Aldolphus walked quietly down the steps, took a seat on the fourth step, and slowly peeked around the wall into the living room. His heart sank into a black abyss as his eyes fixed on the scene before him. Sofia was stark naked, tied to a chair, with her face and body covered in bloody gashes and the beginnings of bruises. A large man, with a bullwhip and what looked like razors attached to it, stood over her. He wore dark sunglasses and a white Stetson hat. The other man was short and stocky, with dark curly hair. He had a chubby face and spoke with a thick Italian accent.

"You've been telling me that same thing for two months now, Clevio," he said.

"I know, Sonny. Just give me another week," said Clevio, as tears ran down his face.

Sonny chuckled, then looked at the man with the bullwhip and nodded. He raised the whip and swung it across Sofia's bare breasts. Blood spurted out of her body instantly and raced down her stomach.

She screamed, "You're killing me! Please stop!" She looked around wildly, and when her eyes met Aldolphus's, she screamed, "Run, baby, run! Get away while you still can!"

Sonny turned and looked at the small boy and grinned maniacally. He walked over to Clevio and grabbed him by his hair. Sonny turned and looked Aldolphus in his eyes and, in one motion, glided the blade across Clevio's throat. Blood sprayed Sonny's face as he dropped the limp body to the floor.

"Run, Aldolphus!" screamed Sofia, as her tears flowed freely down her face.

Aldolphus froze. He couldn't believe his parents were being slaughtered right before his eyes. Sonny walked over and grabbed Sofia by her hair.

"It's your husband's fault," he said with a smile. "And I always thought you were so beautiful, Sofia. I'm sorry," he said, as he swung the bloody razor across her throat. Blood flowed everywhere and a gurgling sound could be heard.

Aldolphus got to his feet and raced back up the stairs toward his room. He heard the rumble of the men's feet behind him. He raised his window and looked out at the ground. It appeared to be a huge drop.

"I got you now, you little bastard!"

Aldolphus turned around and saw Sonny standing in the doorway. He swung his little legs out of the window and held onto the windowsill. Sonny reached out the window and grabbed the child's wrist.

"I'm gonna kill you, you little bastard!" he rasped.

Aldolphus sank his teeth into Sonny's hand as hard and deep as he possibly could. Sonny let out a roar that could match an anguished lion and instantly drew his hand away. Aldolphus dropped to the ground, landing on his bottom. He got to his feet and raced into the shadows of the night.

CHAPTER 2

THE NIGHT AIR WAS COLD and breezy as Aldolphus ran down the now deserted Crenshaw Boulevard. His bare feet were numbed by the freezing earth. Every time a car would pass, the small child would run to hide behind the nearest car for fear of being caught by his parents' murderers. He would never forget the face of the man known as Sonny—his devilish smile and the dark eyes that seemed to pierce the very soul—he would forever be Aldolphus's nightmare.

He thought of his mother's last words: "Run, baby, run!" Her tear-streaked face, and her bloodied body. He thought of the large man with the bullwhip and its sound as it sliced his mother's flesh. In the inner-city streets of Los Angeles was a lost, terrified, and lonely boy with no mother or father; a child that had just seen his life destroyed in minutes; a lost soul walking the quiet streets of death, not knowing the fate of tomorrow.

As he approached a darkened alleyway, he thought briefly about turning around and retracing his steps. Wanting to stay out of the sight of passing cars, he headed down the dark path. It was filled with old trash cans, a dirty sofa, and empty beer bottles. Aldolphus took a seat on the filthy sofa, confusion and pain running through his mind in sudden storms. He began sobbing, allowing his warm tears to fall to the earth. He was cold and frightened; the emotions combining to cause a frenzy of trembling.

Suddenly, he heard a scuffling sound near one of the trash cans. The child got to his feet and picked up a small pole from the ground. He heard a loud screech as a large alley cat leaped from under the debris. The cat landed on a windowsill. Aldolphus walked over toward the opening and realized that what was once a window was now an open hole.

He knelt into the darkness of the gloomy building. Curiously, he extended the pole out before him, waving it back and forth to see if something was there. When he realized there was nothing, he looked over his shoulder and down the alley to reassure himself that no one had followed him and swung his small legs into the darkness. Allowing his body to follow, he landed flat on his back, knocking the wind of out of his body. The pole he had held so tightly clattered as it rolled onto the floor. He slowly got to his knees as he struggled to catch his breath.

The warmth of the large room instantly relaxed him. Whatever this place was, he felt it was a place of comfort. Eventually he got to his feet and allowed his eyes to adjust. He saw that he was in a large basement of some sort of abandoned building. He slowly began walking the length of it. Off to his right, he saw a large refrigerator. He slowly walked over and opened it. The light from the inside instantly illuminated the room. He saw there were old car batteries and tires strewn throughout. Off in the far left corner was a small bed with a blanket. The refrigerator was essentially empty except for a small pitcher of water and a half-eaten cheeseburger. Aldolphus, thinking of the rumble in his stomach, grabbed the sandwich and water. He walked over to the small bed and sat to eat. He devoured the sandwich and water in minutes. Feeling the effects of the day, he stretched out on the bed, pulled the blanket over himself, and laid his pole beside him. The softness of the cot surrounded the small child. At that moment, he felt safe and secure as he drifted off into the beautiful arms of sleep.

When Aldolphus awoke, it was to the strong grip of a silhouette.

"What are you doing in my bed?" said the rough voice from the shadows.

Aldolphus looked up, trying to see the face from which the voice came. One thing the child did notice was the dirty trench coat and gloves the man wore. His odor was that of someone who hadn't bathed in months. The man tightened his grip around the child's throat. Aldolphus began gasping for air. He reached over and grabbed the pole as tightly as he could. Then, in one motion, swung it across the man's face. The sound of bones cracking filled the large room. Aldolphus jumped from the bed. Out of total fear and hysteria, he hit the man repeatedly with the pole. Blood gushed from the bum's head, and in moments, Aldolphus had exhausted himself. He sank to the floor beside the motionless body of the bum. The child's breathing was heavy against the emptiness of the room.

Slowly, Aldolphus got to his feet and headed toward the window. A powerful force from behind brought him to the floor. The bum had taken ahold of his ankle. Instantly, a flood of fear enveloped the child. He saw the familiar devilish smile, those deep piercing eyes, and that chubby face. Then, the voice, that eerie, frightening voice: *I'm gonna kill you, you little bastard.* Aldolphus smashed the bum in the face with his pole as hard as he could. The man's face now looked like a piece of cherry Jell-O.

The child had totally lost control. His vision of the bum was actually of the man responsible for his parents' deaths. Aldolphus continued to bludgeon the body until there was not an ounce of life left. He stood staring at the body. Blood had streaked his face and feet. He dropped the pole and backed away from the body toward the window. He was overcome with fear. In seconds, he was back in the darkness of the deserted alleyway. He raced up the path and out into the street, as fast as his legs would take him.

He was running from the demons that were to chase him for years to come. He was so unaware of his real surroundings that he did not see the oncoming traffic or the vehicle that would send him into the somber abyss of unconsciousness.

CHAPTER 3

ALDOLPHUS AWOKE TO BLURRED VISION. The pontifica-
tor before him was cloudy as he strained his eyes to focus on the
silhouette that towered over his bed.

"How's the little soldier today? My name is Nurse Eva," said the
salient voice.

As the picture slowly became clearer, Aldolphus saw the beautiful face of Sofia.

"Mama?" he questioned.

"No, sweet child," said the elderly black woman as she sat on
the bed beside him. "I'm not your mama, but I'm going to take good
care of you," she said, running her fingers through his curly, black
hair. "You're at Saint Joseph's Hospital," she added.

Aldolphus stared at the chubby face before him. "What happened?" he asked in a cracked voice.

Eva gave him a warm smile. "You've been through a great ordeal,
child. You were hit by a car as you ran out into the street. You've been
here for six days. Three of which you spent in intensive care. The
doctors thought you'd die, but I believed in the power of God," she
said as she grasped the cross that hung from her thick neck. "And I sat
with you and prayed for you for hours. And now, look at you! You're
alive and on your way to recovering." She finished with a smile.

"Did they catch the guy with the whip?" Aldolphus asked
curiously.

"What guy with the whip?" asked Eva worriedly.

"The men that were at my house! The men that killed my mom
and dad! The men with the scary faces!" he cried. Tears began to
travel down his cheeks as Eva embraced the quivering child. She
rocked him gently in her arms back and forth, back and forth.

"I know it hurts, baby. God, I know it hurts."

The door to the room opened, and in walked a uniformed police officer. He was youthful and appeared very eager. He reminded Aldolphus of one of those California surfers. The officer took off his hat and walked to the edge of the bed.

"I'm sorry to intrude, ma'am, but I need to ask the kid some questions," he said mildly.

"This is not a good time," said Eva, still cradling the child in her arms.

Amazingly, Aldolphus spoke, "What do you want? Where were you when those men were chasing me? Where were you when they killed Mama and Daddy?" he sobbed.

It took about an hour for the young officer to gather all the information he could about the killers and the bum. Aldolphus was exhausted after all the questions and immediately drifted off to sleep.

As the days passed and the weeks grew older, Aldolphus began to like St. Joseph's Hospital. Eva became like a second mother to the boy. He loved her for her caring.

She watched over him every day as his therapy instructor made him walk one lap around the hospital perimeter. It was only a matter of days before he was walking again, still with a slight limp but not extremely noticeable. Eva brought him homemade cookies and milk almost every day. They would spend time playing cards, or Eva would teach him some old card tricks. On his birthday, she baked him a cake and sang "Happy Birthday" to him.

One early afternoon, while they played a card game called Speed, they were interrupted by the presence of J. D. Roberts, the senior director of the hospital. Roberts was a stone-faced tall man in his late forties who presented himself with respect and dignity. He stood at the foot of Aldolphus's bed and waited patiently until the game was finished.

"How are you feeling today, Aldolphus?" he asked in a pleasant voice.

"I'm okay," the child responded, not looking up from where the cards lay. "Let's play again, Eva," he said, smiling at her.

Roberts walked around the side of the bed. "Excuse me for a moment, Eva," he said, gently placing his hand on her shoulder.

She slowly got to her feet and backed away from the bed. Roberts took a seat. Aldolphus looked at Eva, then at Roberts. "What's wrong?" he asked curiously.

Roberts took a deep breath. "Aldolphus, your recovery at St. Joseph's has proven to be exceptional, and usually, after a patient's health improves, we send them home." He continued, "But seeing the depths of your misfortunes, we've arranged for you to go to a nice, comfortable home."

"Where? With Eva?" Aldolphus asked excitedly. There was an empty space in the air. Aldolphus looked into Eva's soft brown eyes. *She looks sad,* he thought.

"I'm afraid not," said Roberts. "There is a place affiliated with this hospital. It is called St. Joseph's for Children. It is a place where children stay until the staff are able to find adequate foster homes for them." He finished, watching the child closely.

"I don't want to go to foster care," Aldolphus cried as tears formed into crystal pools in his eyes. "I want to stay with Eva!"

"I'm afraid it's against our rules. I'm sorry, son," Roberts said, getting to his feet. "A van will be here in about an hour to pick you up."

Aldolphus's thoughts were of his father and those dreaded words: *The next time I hear you were anywhere near Airstead Gaddafi, you are going to foster care.*

Foster care. The words repeated themselves in the boy's frightened mind. Eva walked over and took a seat on the bed as Roberts left the room.

"I don't want to leave you, Eva!" he sobbed. Eva held the child in her arms as her own tears raced down her cheeks. "I love you so much, Ms. Eva. Please don't let them take me away! Please!" he begged.

The child's words cut through her like a knife, for she knew there was nothing she could do to stop the young boy's departure. "Oh, I love you, too, dear child," she said, rubbing her fingers through his hair. Eva caressed his small face between her palms and kissed his cheeks gently. "I have something for you," she said, removing the gold diamond-studded cross from around her neck. She placed the large cross over the boy's head. "With this, we'll always be together. Whenever you have a problem, hold onto this real tight and pray to God. He'll answer your prayers," she said softly.

Aldolphus grabbed ahold of the cross and studied it closely. "It's beautiful, Ms. Eva," he said, looking into her eyes.

"My great-grandmother gave it to me before she died, and now I'm giving it to you," she said, slightly bowing her head. Aldolphus hugged her neck tightly.

The door opened, and two large men wearing white uniforms entered. "We're here to pick up Aldolphus Jackson," said one of the men.

Aldolphus knew this would be the start of a new life. He felt pain enter his brain in sudden storms, as he realized he was living in a land full of countless threats and empty promises.

As the van pulled out of the large parking lot of St. Joseph's Hospital, Aldolphus cried silently as Eva waved goodbye. Deep within his heart of hearts, he knew that one day he'd have to return to St. Joseph's to tell Eva how much he truly loved her. He was confused, not knowing what his future held.

CHAPTER 4

ST. JOSEPH'S FOR CHILDREN WAS a large brick building located in the hills behind a blanket of trees. The institution's facade resembled the Catholic cathedral; the windows had painted murals of Jesus Christ with adorning cherubs before his feet. Aldolphus stared out into the cloudy sky and wondered if Sofia and Clevio were looking down on him with shame for not acting like a man. He knew what Clevio would say, "Stop acting like a pussy! Stand up and be a man, which you were born to be…" The words trailed off and buried themselves in the cemetery of the child's memories. The van came to a halt at the entrance of the building.

"We're here," said the driver, looking in the rearview mirror, at the child. As they entered the facility, Aldolphus noticed that the interior resembled a small school. There were classrooms and a recreation room that could be seen from where they stood. All the staff members wore white uniforms and black shoes. Two men led Aldolphus into a large office and told him to take a seat. As the door shut, he drank in the beauty of the immaculately decorated room. There were beautiful paintings of waterfalls on the wall behind the large oak desk. It took only moments before the door opened, and in walked a tall, slim gentleman who appeared to be in his midsixties. He had a large beak-like nose, and the crown of his head was empty; the little hair that he did possess outlined his large ears. He took a seat behind the desk and spoke with a sharp accent, "Hello, Mr. Jackson. Welcome to St. Joseph's for Children. I'm Dr. Roark, the institution psychiatrist. What I'd like to do is conduct a few tests, if you feel up to it."

There was a pause as Aldolphus glared at the man without speaking.

"Did you hear me, son?" He removed his glasses from his nose, then crossed his arms. The child still gave no response as moments passed. "That's fine with me," he said, getting to his feet. "The faster you get with the program, the faster you could possibly get out of here," he stated as he walked toward the door. "Find your way to the rec room." He finished as he closed the door.

Aldolphus got to his feet slowly and walked out into the large hallway. In the distance, he could hear the loud laughter of the other children. As he turned into the large room, he noticed it was equipped with ping-pong and pool tables. The large-screen television was showing an episode of *The Three Stooges*. Aldolphus took a seat in the corner, where he found an empty beanbag. Some of the children spoke, while others didn't. He crossed his arms over his knees and bowed his head.

His thoughts immediately returned to his parents who were brutally murdered over a piece of green paper called *money*. The faces of the killers danced in his mind and caused the small child to feel nothing but anger. And for the first time, he wasn't crying and sobbing. He felt mayhem in his heart.

"You're sitting on my beanbag," said a raspy voice that caused the small child to look up into the cute face of a brown-complexioned girl with pigtails. "Well? Ain't you going to get up?" she continued. Aldolphus felt the burning fires of rage about to explode. "Well, I'll tell my boyfriend, Tank. He'll take care of you!" she said, pivoting on her heel. Aldolphus looked on as she walked over and whispered into the ear of a chubby dark-skinned boy. As the two of them approached, Aldolphus felt his heart racing.

"Didn't my girl tell you to get up, chump?" The voice was harsh and rugged. Aldolphus just glared at them both with fire in his eyes.

The room fell silent as the other children looked on. "I'm talking to you, white boy," he said, slapping Aldolphus across the head lightly. That was all it took. Aldolphus leaped to his feet and swung a punch that connected on Tank's jaw, knocking him backward. Aldolphus ran at the boy again. This time Tank picked the smaller child up and slammed him to the ground. A staff member entered the room and immediately began to separate the two children.

"What happened?" he asked, snatching Aldolphus up by the collar.

"It's her fault!" he gestured at the girl with the pigtails.

"What happened, Summer?" asked the man, studying the little girl closely.

"I beat that chump's ass, that's what happened." Tank interrupted.

The staff turned around and gave Tank a slap in the mouth that caused a trickle of blood to form on his lip. "We don't use those words around here," he snapped.

"You didn't have to hit him," said Aldolphus, lunging at the man.

With one hard push, the man sent Aldolphus flying to the floor. The other children started yelling and screaming obscenities as five more staff members entered the room.

"All right, you two, let's go!" yelled a large man as he snatched both Tank and Aldolphus by the backs of their shirts and headed out of the room. "You both have earned yourselves early bed for three days," he said. He led the kids into a large room that resembled a boot camp dorm, then walked out, closing the door behind him.

Aldolphus walked over and took a seat on one of the beds. Tank paced back and forth for a few moments, then flopped down beside Aldolphus.

Tank broke the silence. "So what's your name, man?" He looked at Aldolphus seriously.

"Aldolphus Jackson," he responded dryly.

"Well, I'm Tank, but I guess you knew that already." Tank shifted his feet. "So why did you stick up for me back there?" he asked curiously.

"I don't know. I guess it was out of anger."

"Hey, you socked me pretty good," he said, rubbing his jaw with a smile.

Aldolphus chuckled. "Yeah, and you slammed me pretty good." He looked at Tank.

"Hey, man, I'm sorry, but my pop always said I should stick up for my lady."

Aldolphus laughed. "Well, my mom always told me I was too young to have a girlfriend."

Tank looked astonished. "You mean you never had a girlfriend?" he asked curiously.

Aldolphus shook his head shamefully.

"Well, it's okay. We can still be friends." Tank placed his hand on Aldolphus's shoulder.

"So how long have you been going with Summer?"

Tank's smile became wide. "Two days." He raised his chest proudly.

Aldolphus laughed harder this time.

"Hey, where'd you get that necklace?" Tank asked.

Aldolphus caressed it tightly in his palm. "I got it from a second mama." His voice was in the low monotone.

"Your second mama? What happened to your first one?" Tank saw the seriousness in his new friend's face and quickly turned his smile into a solemn look of curiosity.

"Both of my parents were killed," Aldolphus blurted out.

Tank shook his head. "My pops was killed too. But Mama is still around," he added.

Aldolphus looked at him. "So why are you here? I thought this place was for kids that lost both parents?"

"Ma-my mom ain't nothing but an old shermhead," he responded nonchalantly.

"What's a shermhead?"

Tank frowned. "You don't know what sherm is?" He didn't wait for an answer. "Sherm is some kind of drug that makes you hungry, lose weight."

"How does it do that?" Aldolphus asked.

"I don't know." Tank shrugged. "But I know my mom is real skinny." He finished. "But she's cool because she lets me do whatever I want." He smiled. Aldolphus stretched.

"So how long have you been here?"

"Only four months this time. Before I ran away the first time, I was here for"—there was a long pause as he counted on his fingers—"six months. I was here for six months the first time."

"They don't beat you when you run away?"

"No way, man. They ain't allowed to beat us in here. Only when we go to foster homes. I've been in two already. I ran away from the first one, and in the second one, I hit my foster brother in the head with a broomstick, so they kicked me out."

"I don't want to go to a foster home! I want to see my second mom."

Tank looked at his new friend. "The only way you could do that is to run from here." Aldolphus appeared to be deep in thought.

"I wish I knew how to get to St. Joseph's Hospital from here." His voice was sad.

"Your second mama is in St. Joseph's Hospital?" Tank looked interested. "I can help you get there. I know my way around this place better than anyone."

"Really?" Aldolphus smiled.

"Lights out," came a voice over the loudspeaker as more children entered the dorm.

"I'll see you in the morning," said Tank, getting to his feet and walking in the opposite direction. Aldolphus lay down and sank into the softness of the large bed. Before closing his eyes, his mind lingered on his precious memories of Eva.

CHAPTER 5

AS THE DAYS PASSED INTO weeks, Aldolphus and Tank became the closest of friends. They did every activity together. Aldolphus taught Tank how to play three-card blind, while Tank taught Aldolphus how to play cee-lo, a popular dice game. During rec time, a Halloween special episode of *Fat Albert* was playing on the television. Dr. Roark entered the room and turned it off.

"Hey! What did you do that for?" snapped Tank, getting to his feet and heading toward the television.

"I'm only going to be a minute, son." Dr. Roark placed his palm on the child's chest. "Kids, I have an announcement to make: one of our family members will be leaving us tomorrow." He smiled. All the children looked around at one another curiously. "Aldolphus, you're the lucky candidate. A nice family has agreed to take you in. Isn't that great?" He clapped his palms together.

Aldolphus felt his heart drop, and a lump formed in his throat. *Not again. You're not sending me away again,* he thought. He looked over at Tank and saw the sadness enter his friend's face. Tank had become like a brother, someone he trusted and cared.

His childhood had become full of misery and filled with dark spots and blank corners.

CHAPTER 6

"LIGHTS OUT, BOYS," CAME THE voice as the children entered the dorm. Aldolphus had been sent up to the dorm early to pack for his long trip to meet his new family. He sat motionless on his bed.

Tank approached. "I'm going to miss you, Aldolphus." He took a seat beside his friend.

"I'm going to miss you, too, Tank."

Tank looked at his friend with watery eyes. "My dad taught me a little saying before he died. It's about friendship. He said him and his best friend would say it to one another when times were rough." There was a quick pause. Tank gripped Aldolphus's hand tightly. "Remember these words: One for all, back to back, until God finds a way for a true soldier. Friends for life." He finished as a tear escaped his eye.

"Yeah, friends for life," Aldolphus responded, trying to blink back the burning waters in his own eyes.

Tank got to his feet, pivoted, and headed toward his bed. Suddenly he stopped and turned on his heel, facing Aldolphus. It was as if both boys knew what the other was thinking. Aldolphus rose as Tank approached. The two children embraced and squeezed one another tightly for what seemed like an eternity, both feeling and understanding their friendship, knowing the difference between dreams and nightmares.

As the black night became somber, the moon cast a ghostly shadow in through the window. Aldolphus found himself sleeping in short, restless periods as fatal thoughts of bloodshed made him sit up in the bed. A mist of sweat covered his body, and Sofia's screams still echoed in his mind. He got out of his bed and headed toward Tank, who was staring at the ceiling, appearing to be in some sort of trance.

"What's up, man? You look scared!" He got to his elbows.

Aldolphus took a seat on the bed and rubbed his fingers through his thick curls. "Can you help me get out of here tonight? I can go find Eva." He spoke in a whisper.

"Are you sure that's what she would want too?" Tank swung his legs off the side of the bed.

"I'm sure," he said with pure intensity. Tank reached for his clothing and began to dress. "Why are you getting dressed? I just want you to help me get out of here."

"We're friends for life, right? So we gotta stick together. I'm going with you." Tank finished, smiling.

"Man, you are one crazy dude!"

"Sshhh." Tank gestured by placing his index finger to his own lips. "Go and stuff your blanket with clothes so that it looks as if someone is sleeping in your bed," Tank whispered.

As Aldolphus headed toward his bed, he heard the rattling of the doorknob. He pivoted to give a signal to Tank, but he had already crawled into his bed and pulled the blankets over himself.

Aldolphus dived for his bed and landed on it seconds before the night staff on duty entered the room with a flashlight and shined it into the eyes of the child. He felt his heart racing, and the butterflies in his stomach ran rapidly. The staff continued to walk the length of the large dorm, then retraced his steps. As the door shut, Aldolphus let out a sigh of relief, knowing that he had been only seconds away from being caught.

Aldolphus quickly got to his feet and dressed himself, then filled his empty bed with clothing and headed toward Tank. He noticed that Tank had tied several sheets together.

"This is our rope. We are going out the window," Aldolphus said seriously.

"That's right. Now help me tie this to the bed," he said as he handed Aldolphus part of the sheet.

"Where you guys going?" came a voice from the darkness. Startled, Aldolphus and Tank both looked up into the face of a blond boy with glasses. "You guys are running away, aren't you? I'm telling!" he snapped.

Both boys got to their feet. "Come on, Jake, please don't tell on us. We'll give you whatever you want!" Aldolphus's voice steeped with urgency.

"Okay, I'll take five dollars from both of you," he said, putting out his hand and smiling devilishly. The two friends exchanged glances.

Tank reached into his pocket. "Okay, here," he said, swinging a hook at the small boy. The power from Tank's fist knocked the boy to the floor. "Cover his mouth!" Tank ran over to the compartment under his bed. Aldolphus straddled the smaller boy and placed both palms over his mouth. When Tank returned, he was carrying two pairs of dirty sweat socks. He knelt beside Aldolphus, grabbed Jake's face, squeezed his cheeks until his mouth opened, then quickly stuffed a stock into it. "Tie his feet." He tossed Aldolphus one of the socks.

After bounding the boy, Tank lifted him by his collar. As tears streamed down Jake's face, Tank forced him across the room and into one of the closets.

"Let's get out of here." Aldolphus lifted the window. Tank dropped the sheet-rope out of it and made sure the end landed close enough to the ground before he climbed upon it and started descending toward the ground. Aldolphus followed closely behind.

Tank began gesturing. "Come on, man, hurry up!"

Back in the facility, the closet door swung open and out ran a hysterical Jake. "Runaways! Runaways!" he screamed, waking the other children. Aldolphus felt his small arms trembling as he hurried to climb down the rope.

"Hurry up, man! Staff are coming!" Tank yelled. Aldolphus looked up and saw that one of the staff had grabbed ahold of the sheet and began pulling. "Jump!" Aldolphus let go of the makeshift rope and fell to the ground. Tank helped him to his feet. "Let's go!" He pulled Aldolphus by the arm, and the two children raced into the depths of the wooded area.

"Where are we?" Aldolphus asked after moments of silence between the two. Tank came to a halt alongside a tree. His breathing was heavy, and his body was feeling tired.

"We're almost at my hideout," he said between breaths.

"Where's your hideout?"

"Remember when I told you about my mom? Well, she lives only a few minutes down the road in the Danger Wood projects. We can hide there until tomorrow and then go find Eva."

The Danger Wood projects were made up of two-story, gray-colored brick houses; some of them were condemned and abandoned. The grounds were polluted with trash and debris, and you could see people hanging out on their porches drinking beer and teenagers in large crowds smoking Swisher Sweet joints, while some of the older hoods stood on corners and sold crack cocaine. The atmosphere took on the look of a place where the future was dim for those who dwelt in its underworld, and the strangers find themselves extinct—tied, gagged, then murdered executioner style.

"What's up, little Tank?" came a voice from the crowd of boys dressed in red. Tank and Aldolphus approached the group of teenagers. A wide smile appeared on Tank's chubby face as he saw a tall, dark-complexioned boy with slanted eyes step from the crowd.

"What's up, Spoony?" he said, slapping hands with the older boy.

"Who's the little white boy?" Smiling, Spoony looked at Aldolphus.

"I'm not a little white boy. My name is Aldolphus Jackson and nothing else," he snapped.

Spoony laughed and looked at the rest of his gang. "Do y'all hear this little motherfucker talking to me like he's a true thug and shit?"

Tank interrupted. "Come on, Spoony, it ain't like that. It's just that my boy has been through a lot of shit."

"I guess I can understand that," Spoony responded, drinking in the picture of his surroundings.

"Look at this motherfucking neighborhood. Everybody around here is walking dead, waiting for their spot under the—" He paused. "Yo! CK! Blaze up one of those swishers." He looked over at a short, light-complexioned boy. CK handed Spoony the cigar filled with marijuana.

"I need your help, Spoony, me and my friend both," said Tank.

There was an empty silence in the air. "I'm listening, little nigga." Spoony blew out a cloud of smoke into the cold air.

"My friend's mama works at St. Joseph's Hospital, and we need a way to get there, so I was hoping you could get us a ride." Tank dropped his eyes to the ground.

Spoony laughed. "Damn, little nigga, is that it? All you got to do is catch one of them ambulances out of here that's carrying one of them dead-ass Crip fools." He laughed harder as the rest of the gang joined in, catching on to Spoony's humor.

"Come on, Spoony, man, I'm serious." You could hear the anger in Tank's voice.

"Look, little motherfucker, don't be catching no attitude with me. If I didn't know your old man, I would leave you hanging. But I'm not because I respect who your pop used to be." He inhaled more marijuana. "Now take your bad ass home and meet me at the Jap store at 3:00 p.m. tomorrow." He turned his back on the small children. Tank glared at him as tears burned his eyes.

"Come on, Tank, let's go," Aldolphus pulled Tank by the arm and headed up the street.

"Damn, Spoony, why you so hard on the little brother?" CK asked in a serious tone. "You just said it. He's my little brother, and the little bastard doesn't even know it." He looked in Tank's direction.

Suddenly, loud screams shattered the night, swelling in volume as they came closer, filling the minds of all who heard with images of death.

"Crip gang motherfucka!" yelled a voice out of the window of the black 1965 Chevy. Bullets spit from the assault rifles that were aimed out of the window.

"Get down!" Tank tackled Aldolphus to the ground. Spoony reached for his weapon but was too slow; the bullet of death was already cutting its way through the cold night. The first one caught him in the shoulder, twisting his body in a circular motion. Before his turn was complete, six more bullets filled his body, leaving him lifeless as he fell to the ground. CK tried to return fire but the Beretta 9 mm that he carried wasn't enough. Three bullets struck him in the face, leaving him with only half a nose and mouth. The rest of the gang scattered like roaches in different directions, fleeing the scene.

Aldolphus tried to get to his feet but was pulled back to the ground by Tank. "Stay down until it's over!" he snapped. The car sped by and made a sharp turn, then disappeared into the night.

Tank got to his feet and began racing toward the bloody murder scene. Aldolphus followed. "Where you going?" He tried to catch Tank but couldn't.

Tank picked up the lifeless head of Spoony. "Wake up, Spoony. Come on," he begged as he shook the lifeless body. You could hear the sirens fast approaching in the distance.

"Come on, Tank. The cops are coming." He pulled Tank to his feet. Both boys raced from the bloody scene.

Here in the underworld of the ghetto streets were two children trapped in a maze of confusion, neither one knowing the destiny of tomorrow. But both prayed silently for brighter days.

CHAPTER 7

"TURN HERE." TANK PULLED ALDOLPHUS onto a dark street.

"I'm sorry about Spoony."

Tank didn't respond. After a few blocks of walking in silence, Tank spoke, "Here's my mama's house."

They walked up the broken concrete steps from the outside. One could see that no lights were on.

"Maybe your mama went out."

Tank took a deep breath. "No way, man. She's here. She's just sittin' in the dark probably cryin' about my daddy." Tank reached for the doorknob.

Aldolphus grabbed his wrist. "How do you know?"

"Because I know my mama." Tank pushed the door open. As they entered, you could smell the aroma of old greens. Aldolphus turned his nose up in anguish. "Come on." Tank led the way across the room to a connecting door. Aldolphus noticed the sofa, which was filled with holes and a dirty pair of tennis shoes. Tank snatched open the door. The room was illuminated only by the fiery glow of a candle.

At the dining room table sat a dark-complexioned woman. Her hair stood on end, and her beautiful slanted eyes looked red and worn by sorrowful and stressful times; her full lips and chiseled nose were untouched by the years of drug use.

"Oh, Clyde!" she said, getting to her feet and running toward Tank. She pulled him close to her bosom and rubbed her fingers through his course hair. Aldolphus looked on. His crystal-blue eyes were like mirrors reflecting short segments of once upon a time. He grabbed ahold of his necklace and said a silent prayer.

"Oh, Clyde, I've been missing you. I was getting ready to go downtown and see the judge about getting back custody of you." She squeezed her son tightly. Tank wiggled his way out of the woman's grasp.

"You always say that, Mama. You been saying the same thing since Daddy died." He turned on his heel and ran out of the room.

Aldolphus stood frozen.

"Oh my." She brought her palms up to her mouth in astonishment. She looked at Aldolphus. "He's not like that all the time, just when he thinks about his dad," she concluded nonchalantly. "So what's your name, Blue Eyes?" She knelt in front of Aldolphus and caressed his small face between her palms. Her gesture brought to life deep and precious memories of Sofia and their last days together. The child blushed.

"Aldolphus Jackson," his response sounded shy.

"That's a nice name, and you're such a cute one too." She pinched his cheeks.

"Well, my name is Grace Williams. You can call me Grace, okay?" Aldolphus nodded.

"What are you doing talking to her? That bitch ain't nothing but a shermhead!" Tank's voice was loud and obnoxious as he entered the room.

Grace got to her feet and slapped Tank hard one time across the face. "Clyde Williams, you'll never talk to your mother that way in her own house!"

Tank rubbed his cheek. "That's why I'm not living here now! All you want to do is beat me. I hope you die! I wish I was never born!" He turned on his heel and pulled Aldolphus along.

Aldolphus turned and looked back at Grace as she sank to the floor, covering her face with both palms. Tank's upstairs bedroom was filled with dirty clothes and junk. The smell of mildew danced in the small room like a relentless spirit. Aldolphus opened his eyes to the bright sun creeping in through the shadeless window. A new day had arrived. He got up from the floor where he had been sleeping for a few short hours. He glanced at Tank, who was sound asleep stretched out on the bed.

He walked over to the window and gazed out into the polluted and eerie projects where just the night before he found himself only fifteen feet away from death. Life and reality was a dark skid road filled with so many sharp turns and unpredictable encounters—a perfect hell that was, in this crazy place, called the world. So many innocent people died here, and so many people were left without mothers and fathers; others were left wearing the cape of guilt as they faded from the scenes of murder.

Thoughts of seeing Eva brought a smile to the child's face. He paced back and forth before the window, then walked over and opened the bedroom door. He could smell the freshly fried sausage and eggs in the air. The aroma made his stomach tumble. He walked over and shook Tank.

"Get up. I think your mama is cooking breakfast."

Tank mumbled something, then sat up and stretched. "What time is it?"

"I don't know, but I know it's early. Let's go see if your mama cooked enough for us."

"Damn, man, you greedy as hell." He got to his feet, laughing.

The two boys entered the kitchen. Grace had her hair fixed in an exceptionally beautiful style. The red lipstick she wore accented her lips to perfection. Her beauty was still queenly, and her body looked firm under the tight jeans she wore.

"Good morning, Ms. Grace."

Grace looked at the sausage, then turned around, greeting Aldolphus with a smile. "Good morning, Blue Eyes." She picked up a towel from the counter and wiped her hands. "And how's my little Tank this morning?" She walked over and embraced her son tightly.

"I'm okay," his response was nonchalant.

She knelt before the two boys and took one of each of their hands into hers. "I have a special breakfast planned for my two little men this morning. Now you boys have a seat at the dining room table, and Mama Grace is going to feed you—both of you."

As they headed into the dining room, Tank froze, then pivoted in the direction of his mother. "Mama..." His voice was a soft monotone. Grace turned to face her son. "You look pretty, Mama."

She gave a big smile. "Come to Mama, baby." She opened her arms as Tank raced over and grabbed ahold of his mother tightly; tears streamed down his chubby cheeks.

"I love you, Mama. I'm sorry about what I said last night."

"It's okay, baby. Mama loves you. Mama loves you very, very much." She caressed him and wiped away his tears, then knelt before her son. "Can Mama have a kiss?" She puckered her lips. Tank leaned over and gently kissed her and headed toward the dining room.

Aldolphus had already taken a seat at the large wooden table.

"You all right, Tank?"

"I guess so." He sat down.

Grace entered the room, carrying a large bowl filled with sausage and eggs. After setting the table, she took a seat and watched the two children devour the hearty meal. "Have you boys had enough?"

"Yes, Mama, I sure miss your cooking." Tank smiled.

"How about you, Blue Eyes?"

"Yes, ma'am, I've had more than enough."

Suddenly, knocks on the door interrupted the conversation.

"Can I use the bathroom, Miss Grace?"

"Sure, honey, use the one in the basement." She got to her feet and headed to the dining room.

"Don't fall in the toilet." Tank antagonized his friend before laughing.

As Aldolphus entered the dusty basement, he could hear voices from upstairs. The volume began to rise suddenly; then he heard screams followed closely by what sounded like a scrap taking place. The floor shook like a thunderclap. Aldolphus raced up the stairs, then opened the door slowly. Through the small crack, he could see that Tank was being handcuffed by a police officer and pinned to the floor.

You could see tears running down Tank's face as he screamed to no avail, "Let me go, let me go!"

"Take them fucking handcuffs off my son!" Grace appeared in the doorway, standing akimbo.

"Look, ma'am, this child was in the custody of the state. Now I suggest that you tell me where the other one is hiding before I am forced to take you downtown." The officer got to his feet and pulled Tank up by the collar. Aldolphus backed slowly away from the door, then crept slowly down the wooden steps one at a time. He thought momentarily about hiding in the basement, but he knew the officer would search the house. He didn't want to leave Tank, but at the same time, his sweet memories of Eva were calling him.

He climbed on top of the old toilet and quietly opened the window. The cold air entered, instantly touching his face. He climbed out into the backyard and got to his feet, then peeked into the kitchen window. He could tell from Grace's gestures that she and the officer were engaged in a heated debate. He turned and began to put distance between himself and the old house.

The farther he ran, the more he began to regret it. He and Tank were like brothers; breaking their bond of friendship was the last thing he wanted to do. They had been through a storm of hard times together, but the biggest question for the confused child was this: When would the sun return to illuminate his dark and dreary days? Throughout the shattered and empty life of this ghetto child, the dark streets had taken away four of his loved ones: two by the way of death, and two by the way of separation.

He felt the pain in his right leg where the car had struck him, but he kept running. Determination had now become a part of the child's everyday life. Tank's words echoed in his mind, *Back to back, until God finds a way for a true soldier.*

Aldolphus continued to run until he came upon a house that looked abandoned. His breathing was heavy as he walked onto the porch. The police sirens sounded as if they were getting closer. He turned the knob, then entered, closing the door just enough to see outside. At that moment, two police cruisers sped by. He shut the door completely, then leaned his back against it, hoping they had not noticed him. Suddenly he heard the muffled sound of voices that seemed to be coming from the back of the house. Curiosity sparked in his heart and began guiding his small legs toward the sounds. He froze, suddenly having second thoughts, but as the voices became louder, the child's mind told him to continue.

The floors in the old house were wooden, making every step that he took a creaking one. As he approached the door, he could hear loud and clear the laughter of people from behind it. He reached for the knob slowly, not quite knowing what he would find. He turned the knob and pushed the door open. The last thing he remembered was seeing the large guns being pointed at him from three boys dressed in red. Then he fainted.

Moments later, his eyes fluttered open, and he found himself looking at three faces.

"What happened?" he asked as one of the teenagers help him to his feet.

"You fainted, little man. We thought you were one of those Bloods trying to set trip, so we pulled our shit. Ready to blast on you, then you passed out." He chuckled.

Suddenly Aldolphus realized that these were the gang members that were with Spoony.

"So where is little Tank?" asked one of them.

"The cops caught him."

"What have y'all li'l niggas done now?"

"We ran away from the shelter. I was trying to get to St. Joseph's Hospital to visit Ms. Eva, but Tank told me that we could spend the night at his house and that Spoony would take us today, but then Spoony got shot."

"Hold up, little man. Don't even lay the jive on us, man," said one boy speaking for the first time.

"Come on, DJ, lay off the young buck." The boy's voice was firm.

"Fuck that shit, Eddie Boo. That little nigga knows too much. What if the cops catch him and he starts talking, then we are all assed out." He glared at Aldolphus.

"I'm not a snitch!"

"You little bastard. I should slap the shit out of you for talking to me like that." DJ lunged toward the child.

Eddie Boo stepped in front. "DJ, cool out, baby boy. Remember that little boy is affiliated with Tank's family, which makes him family."

DJ glared at his friend, then back at Aldolphus. "Yo, dice man, come on. It's your turn to shoot."

He focused his attention on the kid with the dice. "I am seven eleven tonight, motherfuckas," he said, rolling the dice.

DJ laughed. "You crapped out, my nigga. It's my turn," said Eddie Boo, picking up the dice.

Aldolphus looked on from behind the small cipher that had been formed around the money. Eddie shook the dice, then blew into his fist. "I am hot tonight, baby. Y'all niggas better quit now. I already broke you suckers for two stacks."

Eddie turned and looked at the Aldolphus. "Come here, little man. You want to roll these for me?" He handed the child two dice. Aldolphus entered the cipher and shook the bones like a true professional. DJ and Dice looked at one another and smiled. Aldolphus rolled the dice. They hit the wall and flipped a few times and stopped.

"Seven! Yeah, youngblood!" exclaimed Eddie, jumping to his feet. "This game is over." Eddie knelt and scooped up the pile of green backs. He peeled off a twenty-dollar bill and handed it to Aldolphus. "Good roll, young boy." He placed the money in his pocket.

A small beeping noise filled the room. Eddie pulled the pager from his belt and looked at it. "Booty call," he said, laughing. "I will see you cats later. Take it easy, little man," he said before walking out of the room. Aldolphus followed behind.

"Where are you going, little man?" DJ asked.

"I'm going to St. Joseph's Hospital."

"I'll give you a ride, but you got to do me a favor," DJ said, getting to his feet. The thought of someone finally giving him a ride turned him into a thousand smiles.

"Okay, I will do whatever. Just take me there."

Dice looked at DJ, curious before speaking, "Well, I'm going to check on my baby mother." He turned on his heel and left the room. "Come on, little man." DJ put his arm around the child and headed out of the room.

The early afternoon clouds glided slowly across the sky, indicating that a storm was fast approaching.

"You know anything about crack cocaine?" DJ asked as they walked down the back alley of the projects.

"No, but I've heard of it. Isn't that the stuff on the television commercial that says, 'This is your brain on drugs?'"

DJ chuckled. "You got the idea, young buck. I can see me and you will get along just fine. Wait here." DJ walked into a corner store.

Aldolphus looked around, still nervous about being chased by the police.

DJ returned only moments later. "Check this out, young buck." He pulled out a handful of capsules filled with a white powder. "I want you to put these in your pocket, and when someone wants it, you give it to them, and they will give you ten dollars. Remember I will be here with you, so only sell to the people that I say, okay?"

Aldolphus nodded. The two of them walked farther onto a run-down street that was littered with trash and condemned buildings. The walls were spray-painted with *RIP* and *in memory of* writings. DJ relaxed against a wall.

"Don't look so nervous, young buck. I ain't gonna let nothing happen to you, and besides that, my connect is on his way, and he has enough shit to supply this whole damn city. Who knows, if you act right, he might even take you under the wing."

Aldolphus felt nauseous and early signs of diarrhea bubbling in his stomach. Something about DJ made him nervous.

A man wearing an old overcoat and dingy skullcap approached. "You got anything?" His voice trembled.

Aldolphus looked afraid. "Chill out, young buck. It's only a dope fien'."

Aldolphus looked into the man's face. His eyes were bloodshot red, and the skin on his dark face was so tight that you could see his bone structure. Aldolphus reached into his pocket and pulled out one of the capsules and handed it to the man. He took it and handed the child a ten-dollar bill.

"See how easy that was?" DJ took the money from the child's hand. As the minutes passed, the traffic of people increased. DJ directed each person to Aldolphus, who was now selling the caps like a true professional.

Suddenly, loud vibrations of music coming from a black Cadillac with tinted windows caught the child's attention. The car approached slowly and pulled up alongside the curb. The gold Daytons sparkled under the afternoon sun that peeked from behind the somber clouds.

"That's my connect." DJ got to his feet.

The door to the Cadillac opened, and out stepped an immaculately dressed man; he wore a pair of alligator shoes, a tailor-made purple Armani suit, and a black-rimmed Homburg hat. As Aldolphus met eyes with the man before him, the deep blue-crystal color of the man's piercing eyes sent a shiver of recognition throughout his body.

It was him. It had to be. The man who had treated him with so much gentle kindness and affection; the man who had waited outside his elementary school and gave him fifty dollars. Airstead Gaddafi was his name; Aldolphus was sure of it.

"Mr. Airstead," he blurted. DJ looked in the child's direction, curious.

Airstead approached DJ. "What the fuck is this shit?" He grabbed DJ by the collar.

"What are you talking about, man. Cool out!" Airstead slapped him viciously across the face, then pulled out a chrome .357 Magnum and put it to DJ's head.

"Cool out! Is that what you say to me? Cool out! How can I cool out when you have babies out here selling your shit?" Aldolphus looked on; his small heart pounding in his chest and stomach doing flips.

"Empty your pockets, motherfucker, now!" he snapped, cocking back the hammer of his gun. DJ reached in his pocket and pulled out a large bankroll of money and dropped it to the ground.

"Pick it up, Aldolphus," commanded Airstead, gesturing toward the large bankroll.

How does he know my name? the child thought. He knelt and picked up the money.

"Now the next time I catch you making little kids sell for you, I'm going to kill you. Is that understood?" he asked, slapping DJ's cheek lightly.

"I'm sorry, Airstead. Sorry, man. It will never happen again. I promise." His voice trembled.

"I know, I know, I know. Don't worry about it, okay. Just don't let it happen again." Airstead turned on his heel.

"Come on, kid. You're going with me." He put his arm around the child and walked toward his car. Aldolphus glanced at the shiny gun that Airstead held in his hand.

Suddenly the man called Airstead turned swiftly and fired two shots, both cutting through DJ's body with a heated fury so intense that it took a moment for the boy to realize that he was on his way to meet God at heaven's gate. His body dropped to the pavement, and blood flowed freely from it. Aldolphus stood staring at the lifeless body, almost appearing comatose by what had just happened.

Airstead placed the gun back into his jacket. "Let's go," he said calmly, then got into the car.

Aldolphus jumped into the passenger seat. Airstead pulled onto the street, then made a quick right turn at the corner. Rain began to fall slowly at first, then increased rapidly. Airstead stopped at a red light, then looked at Aldolphus.

"Are you always this quiet?" He smiled.

"I'm just afraid after seeing you shoot that guy back there."

"You have no reason to be afraid of me. I shot that kid over you. I know all about what happened to your mother and father, and hopefully never have to worry about that sort of thing happening again, but when you're dealing with those sorts of kids, anything can happen."

"How do you know so much about me and my family?"

Airstead chuckled. "There's a lot of things I know that you don't realize that I do. If you hang with me long enough, you will learn the tricks of the trade." The light turned green; then Airstead made a right turn onto a street called Beckwood.

"Why did Mama and Daddy hate you so much?"

Airstead chuckled again. "There's a lot of people that hate me all over the world for different reasons. Some people hate me because I'm rich. Others because they want to be me." He laughed.

"So why did you used to give me money and stuff?"

"Listen, Ice. Do you mind if I call you Ice? I like that name for you. It fits your eyes. How 'bout you? You like that name?"

"I don't care what you call me. I just want an answer to my question," he snapped.

"Listen, Ice, you ask a lot of questions, so here's what I'm going to do. Why don't you tell me what's your biggest wish? And I guarantee I can make it come true."

There was a long pause. Aldolphus studied the man's face closely; his clear blue eyes serious and intense.

"I wish the police would catch the people that killed my mama and daddy."

Airstead nodded in agreement. "Don't worry. Things will happen in time. Always remember, young one, to practice patience."

He rubbed the child's head. Silence enveloped the car, and Aldolphus felt sleep tugging on his eyelids. His final thoughts were scattered between Tank and their broken friendship and realizing that Aldolphus was no longer his name. Life has its way of being so cruel to the ghetto.

CHAPTER 8

AS THE CAR CAME TO a halt, the young boy who would become known as Ice consciously knew that the ride had come to an end. He opened his eyes and looked over at Airstead to reassure himself that he was not living in a dream. Airstead lit a cigar, then exhaled a cloud of smoke.

"Do you remember this neighborhood?"

Aldolphus took in his surroundings. Instantly he realized that it was the place that Sofia had told him to stay away from. It brought back memories. It was the BBC Ballroom. A known hangout for gangsters and players. The place where he had studied the gangsters' style: the way they dressed, walked, talked, and acted.

The strip was filled with popular clubs and sleazy porno shops. Prostitutes stood on the corners, and pimps watched from afar. The traffic was like rush hour in the early morning hours. The late afternoon sky was tinted with the slight color of purple, indicating that night was approaching.

"Let's go," Airstead said, getting from the car and walking to the passenger side and opening the door. Ice stepped onto the curb.

A white woman wearing a thick fur coat and lots of makeup approached. "Daddy, I made $500 so far. Can I take a break?" she asked, looking at Airstead.

He looked the girl from head to toe, then grabbed a handful of her blond hair. "Listen here, cheap hooker. If you wanted a day off, you should have become a secretary. Furthermore, don't ever, in your short life, approach me while I'm with this kid." He pointed toward Ice. "Now get your nasty ass back to whore time." He shoved her backward.

"Who was that?" the child asked curiously.

41

"You will learn everything in time." He wrapped his arm around the child. "Do I have a way with women or what?" He laughed.

The outside of the large building resembled an old movie theater; the flashing blue sign on top of the double iron doors read "BBC Ballroom." As they entered the bar, the waitress walked around topless, exposing her breasts to whomever was watching. The loud music bounced off the walls and echoed out. The bar was made of white marble and was oval shaped. Ice looked around and absorbed the atmosphere. Everyone here was equally dressed in expensive jewelry and coats. The child had encountered many things lately but nothing of this magnitude. He felt out of place. Airstead walked up to the bar. The bartender was a boy who looked around twenty-five. He wore a white shirt and a purple bow tie.

"What can I get for you, sir?"

"Give me the norm." Ice looked on as the boy tossed glasses and shook up the drink, then slid it toward Airstead, who picked it up immediately.

"You want some?" He handed the glass toward Ice. The boy took it, then sipped it lightly.

"Yuck! What the fuck is that?" He spat the liquid onto the floor.

Airstead laughed loudly. "It's Ice tea."

"I have never tasted that kind of tea before." He used his forearm to wipe his lip.

Airstead laughed again. "Come on. I have people for you to meet."

They headed toward a pair of spiral stairs. As they reached the top, they entered a long hallway. Both sides had rooms that resembled a motel.

"Where are you taking me?"

"To meet your new family." Airstead pulled out a set of keys as they approached the door with the number 112 above it. The muffled sound of music could be heard coming from the room. Before Airstead could insert the key, the door opened, and there stood a woman with the beauty of an ancient goddess. Ice thought he would faint at the shocking resemblance that she had to his mother, Sofia. Her hazel-brown eyes and thick, full lips were pronounced. She was not as tall as Sofia, but her figure was that of a supermodel, and the black silk dress only complemented this fact. Her complexion was a deep penny rust and looked soft and gentle.

"Hey, honey." She stepped forward and wrapped her arms around Airstead and kissed him with passion. "And look at your little twin." She knelt before the child. "What are we going to call him, honey?"

"I decided on Ice. He responded flatly."

"Oh, I love it." She smiled. "I'm Irene. Can you remember that?" The child nodded.

"Follow me, kid."

Airstead headed through another door. As they stepped into the room, the scene was more explicit than anything the child had seen. Young women were dancing in front of older men who looked like they belonged on wanted posters for pedophilia.

"Where is Shortman?" Airstead asked, looking back at Irene.

"I think he is in the back. I'll get him." She turned on her heel and walked down the hall. Her hips moved side to side with almost a rhythm.

"That's my wife, youngster. Don't look so hard." He chuckled, looking down at Ice. The child laughed.

A nude woman walked over and grabbed the child's hand. "I lost my dance partner. Do you want to take his place?" She pulled the child onto the floor.

He looked back at Airstead nervously. "Go ahead, boy. Have some fun." Airstead laughed.

When Irene returned, she was accompanied by a very short brother of about twenty-five years old. He was brown skinned and dressed in an expensive suit.

"What's up, boss?" He approached.

"Any problems so far?"

"Not at all, boss, but if there is, I have my girlfriend with me." He opened his jacket and displayed the gun in the holster.

Airstead laughed. "Do you see that kid dancing with that red-headed hooker?" He pointed at Ice.

"Yes, I see him."

"Well, I want you to watch over him for me tonight. I have some important business to take care of near the beach, so make the youngster as comfortable as possible."

"It looks like he's having his way already," Irene said, smiling. The redhead was bent over and grinding her backside against the boy's crotch.

"Yes, it looks that way," Shortman said with a chuckle.

"So how much trap money we make so far tonight?" Airstead looked at Irene.

"Well, I was in the back counting everything up when you came in. I don't remember the exact figures, but I know that it's somewhere around $5,000."

"That's pretty good so far. Shut everything down at 4:00 a.m."

"You got it, babe."

"I'll see you tomorrow," he said, kissing Irene softly on the lips, then exited out of the room.

"I guess I better take the youngster in the back with me," said Shortman.

"I don't know. That might be kind of hard to do. Look at him." Irene laughed.

Ice was in full charge, dancing like he was in a popular nightclub; beads of sweat ran down his small face as his little body moved with the music.

"I'll get him." Irene walked onto the floor and took the child by the hand. "You have to go to the back with Shortman. You can finish your dance later, okay?" Her voice was gentle. He followed.

"Are you having fun, little man?" Shortman asked as they approached.

Ice nodded. "Yeah! I haven't danced like that in years."

Irene and Shortman both laughed hysterically. "Oh, listen at you, boy, talking like you're a grown man."

She caressed his cheek. He blushed from embarrassment. "Are you hungry?" she asked.

The thoughts of food sounded good to the child's ears. "Yes, ma'am."

"Oh, honey, you don't have to call me ma'am." She leaned forward and kissed him on the cheek. He blushed again.

"Come with me, Ice." Shortman intervened and headed down the hall toward a film. There were at least a dozen television monitors all displaying various parts of the compound. Ice took in his surroundings in amazement. "Have a seat." Shortman pointed to a large, black leather sofa. Ice took a seat. The softness of the couch surrounded his body. Shortman propped his feet up, then picked up an outdated newspaper and began looking through it.

"Are you a security guard?" He broke the silence.

Shortman chuckled. "Something like that."

"Is this Mr. Airstead's club?"

"You're very curious about a lot, aren't you, youngster? Look, I realize that there is lot of things that you don't understand right now, but as time goes on, Airstead and Irene will make everything clear for you."

"Is someone keeping something from me?"

"Not that I know of, but I think you are aiming your questions in the wrong direction."

Suddenly the door opened, and in walked Irene with a plate of chicken and rice. The aroma filled the room. Ice felt his mouth water as she sat the plate of food in his lap.

"I hope this is enough for you, honey. I had the waiter bring it up fresh out of the pot." Irene took a seat next to him and watched as he devoured half of the food on the plate. "You must've been hungry. I see you have a big appetite for such a little man." She laughed. He smirked.

"Ms. Irene, can I ask you a question?" His expression was serious and intense.

"Sure, honey, you can ask me anything."

"Did you know my mama and daddy?"

"What would give you that idea?"

"Because Mr. Airstead knew them, so I thought you would too."

"Don't get the wrong idea. Airstead only knew your parents through school. After that, he really never saw them much, but after he read about what happened to them in the paper, he immediately tried finding you to avoid you going into foster care."

"But why would he search for me if he had not seen my parents since high school?" Irene exhaled. "Your father Clevio and Airstead were best friends in high school. Your father saved his life once when he was being hunted by gang members. They were actually still friends when you were born."

"Well, what happened then?"

Irene took a deep breath. "Clevio accused Airstead of trying to steal Sofia from him. He and your father had a fight, and they have never spoken since."

The picture was finally becoming clear. Irene continued to talk. He was aware of her voice but not of what was being said. His thoughts had grown legs and traveled back in time to meet with his past: the day Airstead had given him a turkey to take home, or the day he waited for him after school just to give him a crisp fifty-dollar bill. *Was he trying to become friends with my father again? Yes, that had to be it.* Sofia's words echoed off the walls of his brain. *I'm only hard on you because I love you. One day you will understand.* The thoughts trailed off and popped like a tiny soap bubble, bringing him back to reality.

"I'm sorry, Ms. Irene. What did you say?" She chuckled, realizing that the child had been drowning in his own troubled thoughts.

"I said that your father made Airstead promise that no matter what happened between them, that if he was to pass on for whatever the reason, that Airstead would take care of you, so he is keeping his promise." She smiled, showing her perfectly spaced ivory teeth. Ice sat, looking into the softness of Irene's beautiful eyes. He felt safe and secure all at once. But still could not shake the fear and confusion. Haunted by the memories of once upon a time.

Irene got to her feet. "Don't ever bring this conversation up around Airstead." Her tone was serious.

"I promise not to." Irene turned on her heel and left the room.

"You see how easy that was? Now get yourself some sleep. We have a lot of shopping to do tomorrow," said Shortman, getting to his feet and heading toward the exit.

"Thanks, Shortman."

Shortman smiled. "I don't know what you are thanking me for, but whatever it is, you're welcome." He left the room.

Ice sank into the sofa, and it took only moments for sleep to caress his body. He reached and grabbed ahold of the charm that dangled from the chain around his neck.

"I miss you, Eva," he said, then drifted off into the land of dreams.

CHAPTER 9

AIRSTEAD PULLED HIS CADDY IN the front of a rundown apartment building. Darkness had fallen upon the earth, and the early pale moon was struggling to rear its head and cast its ghostly shadow upon everything that lurked in the underworld. Airstead grabbed a small duffle bag off the passenger's seat, exited the vehicle, and headed into the old building. Empty beer cans and other debris could be seen scattered about. He made his way up a pair of old wooden steps that creaked with almost every step that he took, then down a short hallway that creaked equally as much. He rang the bell for apartment B.

A minute passed before the door was opened by a pudgy short white man who looked to be in his late thirties. He had dark brown eyes that matched his curly hair and sported a five o'clock shadow.

"What's up, Spartan?" Airstead shook hands with the man before stepping into the apartment.

"I was starting to think that you would be a no-show," he responded.

Airstead smirked. Spartan's apartment was in immaculate condition. The hardwood floors glossed with a brown stain, and the country-style furniture matched it perfectly. Spartan was an ex-Navy SEAL who had specialized in explosives, but his reputation as a homosexual got him blackballed from the military.

"So what do you have for me?" Airstead rubbed his palms together, then took a seat on the couch.

"One moment." Spartan left the room, then returned with a black briefcase. "You are going to love this." He gently sat the case on the glass table and opened it. It appeared to be empty.

"What kind of a game are you playing, Spartan? Giving me an empty case," he snapped.

"Calm down, calm down. Let me show you the trick." He reached into the case and pulled up a false bottom. "Now, fix your eyes on that work of art."

Airstead studied the wires and grenade-shaped objects closely. "What exactly is it?"

"Plastic explosives with the power to take down one small apartment complex with just the push of a button." He reached into his pocket and revealed a small oval-shaped remote with a large, red button and handed it to Airstead. "All you have to do is turn on the switch and hit the button, and the rest will be in the news."

Airstead gave a devilish grin. "You never cease to amaze me, Spartan."

Airstead replaced the false bottom, then reached into his duffle bag. "How much did we agree on?" Revealing stacks of one-hundred-dollar bills.

Spartan thought a moment. "Fifty thousand dollars, I believe."

Airstead began stacking bills into the briefcase with the false bottom. After covering it, he tossed the duffle bag at Spartan. "That's $150,000 for you. I will be in need of another one of these very soon." He shut the case and got to his feet.

"Do you mind if I use your telephone?"

"Be my guest." Spartan gestured toward the kitchen. Airstead picked up the phone and dialed seven numbers.

The phone rang about four times before a husky voice answered, "Rusty's place."

"Yeah, this is Airstead Gaddafi. I was scheduled to meet with Rusty tonight at nine to discuss some real estate that I was interested in purchasing."

"One moment." The line went silent for a few minutes; then the husky voice returned. "Rusty says be here in a half an hour." And then the line went dead.

Airstead chuckled then checked the time on his watch. It was 7:30 p.m. *The ride to Rusty's would take about ten minutes, so why not get a head start,* he thought, walking through the living room and heading toward the exit door.

"I will be in contact, Spartan." He closed the door behind and made his way down the steps and out to his car.

The full moon had finally broken free from the clouds of darkness. Airstead looked into the sky. "It's a full moon, and the wolf is out. Someone is going to die tonight." He smiled, then started his car. He gently placed the briefcase under the passenger seat, then merged into the shadows.

Airstead was on his way to meet with the godfather of LA: Rusty Santucci. Rusty was feared in many cities across the United States. The kind of man who had been labeled as a true untouchable mob figure. The cops feared him, senators invited him to dinner, and federal agents warned him of indictments. It was rumored that he had cut out the tongue of his own brother for whistling at his wife. Even though he was now sixty-five years of age and suffering from tuberculosis, his presence alone in a room still created sweaty palms and shifty eyes. Airstead realized what sort of evil he was truly facing, but his determination to become what the mob called a "made guy" drove his desire. The last inner-city hoodlum that attempted to negotiate with Rusty was found pumped full of bullet holes and smoking in an alley on mystery night.

These hideous facts danced in Airstead's mind. But deep within his ice-cold heart, he had come to terms with the fact that death in this game of blood rules was somehow his destiny. When Airstead had first been released from prison after five years, he promised himself that he would become a rich man. It didn't take long for him to achieve that. He had become a known and respected real estate tycoon; he owned a beautiful mansion in Las Vegas and a popular ballroom in LA. But Airstead wanted more: he wanted power, respect, money by the truckloads, and women by the dozens. Oh yeah, and law enforcement bowing at his feet. What better way to get to the top than to make Santucci an offer he couldn't refuse?

He realized that his chances of making it out of Rusty's alive was slim, so he figured that if he was going to pass on into the next life, that he wasn't going alone. He smiled to himself, trying to suppress the butterflies fighting in his stomach. He pulled into an empty lot about a block away from Rusty's. He picked up his briefcase, got out of the car, and headed toward the lavish nightclub.

From the outside, it looked like a casino. On the inside, it had three glass dance floors, five bear-skinned bars, and an elegant restaurant area. As Airstead approached the entrance, two men in long overcoats and sunglasses stood in his path.

"He's here, boss," said one of them, speaking into a headset. He stood intently as he received instruction from the other end. "All right, turn around and put your hands on your head."

Airstead felt a lump form in his throat as he sat the case down and followed the man's orders. One of them began frisking him roughly. "Watch the blazer, man. I paid top dollar for this shit."

"Shut up, punk." He nudged Airstead in the back. Airstead took a deep breath, then rolled his eyes up in his head. "All right. Turn around. What's in the case?" he asked, bending over and picking it up. Airstead felt his adrenaline flowing. Getting caught at this moment was the last thing he needed right now. So far, his plan was airtight, but suddenly he could feel a small draft creeping through. The man shook the case from one side to the other. Airstead froze, thinking the bomb would explode at any second. It didn't. *Good job, Spartan,* he thought to himself. He sat the case on the ground and opened it in what seemed almost like slow motion. He stared at its contents intently, then shut it, got to his feet, and handed it to Airstead. "Traveling kind of heavy tonight, I see." His tone was sarcastic.

Airstead chuckled. "That's the only way to travel these days."

He walked past the two men, then entered the club. The restaurant area was dark and only illuminated by a single light dangling over a side booth. Three large Italian men emerged from the shadows. One of the men took hold of his arm.

"Come with us."

They led Airstead behind one of the bars and back into a dark hallway. Airstead thought for certain that the three goons were ready to ambush him at any moment. A side door opened, and out walked another man. He was dressed in black, and his rust-colored hair was in a long ponytail.

"I will take him from here, fellows. Follow me."

As they stepped into the room, it had a red tint, possibly from party bulbs of some sort. In the far corner of the room was a round table, and at it sat four men. None of them were familiar except the eldest one. He had a large beak of a nose, snow-white-colored hair, almost invisible lips, and piercing gray eyes that were evil.

"Have a seat." He gestured in the direction of an empty seat at the table. Airstead walked over, sat the briefcase in the center of the cipher, then took a seat.

"You've got some pretty big balls coming down here, young lad." Airstead allowed his eyes to glide across the faces of the other occupants seated at the table. "So this better be good. I'm in no mood for games tonight. You have five minutes to speak your mind. Anything after that is asking for trouble." Rusty folded his arms and glared at the young upstart.

He cleared his throat. "Look, Mr. Santucci, I didn't come here for trouble. I am merely here to conduct clean-cut business, nothing else." Airstead felt comfortable at his own choice of words.

Rusty laughed, then began coughing uncontrollably. One of the other men began patting him on the back gently. "Are you okay, boss?"

"Of course, I'm okay, you idiot!" He shrugged, showing he was irritable.

"Just who in the hell are you, Airstead? Some sort of clown coming here to amuse me with your slick choice of words?"

"Not at all, sir. I just want it to be known before I go any further that I have come peacefully."

"Continue, continue." Rusty gestured as to be in a hurry.

Airstead cleared his throat again. He knew that his next words had to be airtight and without sign of weakness. "Mr. Santucci, I have with me $10,000 as a gift if you will partner with me by allowing me to join your business. What this city needs, I know you have the power to provide. I have had a contractor design for me a blueprint of a casino. I hope you would review it with a keen eye. It is my wish that you accept me as a partner, demolish this place, and begin construction immediately on a new and improved Santucci Casino and Resorts. Now tell me you can't smell the money." There was a silence.

From the look on Rusty's face, Airstead knew that he had probably failed the test. What would come next would be the heated fury of a diabolical human. "Are you afraid of me, Airstead?" His words were calm at first.

Airstead looked the man in the eye. "My father always taught me to never fear anything in the physical form."

"Your father? Now what can you tell me about Alexas Gaddafi that I don't already know? Your father was a peg leg pussy bitch heroin addict." His voice calmed. "I gave your father a chance to be a millionaire, and you know what he did? The bastard tried to rob me, and now look: the sorry son of a bitch has been missing for years."

Airstead didn't know what precipitated this diatribe, but the newly discovered revelation of what had happened to his father was like a crucifixion. His father had been missing for more than twenty years, and his mother died of a broken heart because of it. The past has a mysterious way of haunting the innocent. Airstead had never truly wanted to know what had happened to his father, but now that he did, he vowed to serve justice by way of blood rules upon his wicked adversary.

"I think I better leave now." Airstead got to his feet.

Rusty laughed. "I would be a true fool if I were to let you walk out of here alive, but then again, you are already dead." He gestured with his hand like a gun. Airstead reached for the briefcase. Rusty slammed his open palm on top of it. "This stays here. Let's just call it a little exchange. The money for your life at the moment, and who knows, you might even live for twenty-four hours." He chuckled.

Airstead took a deep breath. "You know when I told you earlier that I wasn't afraid of any man? Well, I was being untruthful. I fear you, Mr. Santucci." He bowed his head in defeat.

"Get the hell out of my face, punk, before I change my mind." Airstead turned on his heel and retraced his steps.

Once he reached the outside of the club and passed Santucci's security, he knew that it would only be minutes before he would send Rusty's up in flames. The pain of lost loves made his heart tremble with fury and the burning desire for revenge. He reached into his pocket and pulled out his keys.

"Excuse me, sir. Is this your car?" Airstead turned and saw a tall brunette dressed in knee-high boots and a short miniskirt approaching.

"Yes, it is. Who needs to know?"

"What a sorry attitude," she responded, standing akimbo.

"Look, lady, I'm in a hurry, so what can I do for you?"

"Well, nothing really. I just wanted to tell you that I saw a couple of guys fooling around under your car about twenty minutes ago. They didn't look like mechanics to me." Her words hung in the air like they were frozen in time.

"Thanks for the lookout."

"Sure thing, but don't you think that you owe me something for that information?" She held out her palm. In any other circumstance, Airstead would have slapped her across the face, but there was no doubt that Rusty would discover the bomb sooner than later.

Time was crucial. Airstead dropped to a push-up position and scanned the undercarriage of his vehicle. He noticed two red wires connected to a small clock; they traced from the back of the tailpipe and ended at the driver's side door, making it so that whoever opened the door would be blown into the next stratosphere.

That sorry bastard was going to kill me anyway, he thought to himself. Airstead got to his feet.

"You've got to go. This thing is going to blow any second now." The woman backed away slowly at first, then raced in the opposite direction of the street. Airstead pulled out the detonator from his pocket.

"This is for that peg leg addict. Roast in the devil's home, you old son of a bitch," he said through clenched teeth.

Rusty looked around the table. "That dumb bastard is about to be blown to the sky." He laughed. The explosion came in a hot, ghostly fury. Shards of glass scattered as the walls became confetti, and one large mass of fire ran a track meet, killing everything breathing. Smoke clouds drifted toward the heavens, taking with them each man's soul to be judged in front of the Almighty.

Airstead looked on from a distance, wearing the devil's smile. "That's for you, Dad," he whispered.

He walked across the street to a pay phone, then dialed a number. As the phone rang on the other end, Airstead could hear police sirens approaching in the distance.

"Hello."

"Spartan, I need your help."

"What happened?" Spartan questioned.

"It's not what happened. It's what could have happened," he responded.

"Where are you?"

"I'm about two blocks from Rusty's place in the old boxing gym's parking lot."

"I'll be there." Then the line went dead.

CHAPTER 10

THE SONGBIRDS CHIRPED IN PRECIOUS harmony as the sun began to introduce itself to a new day. Ice was awakened by the muffled sound of music. He smiled at himself and oddly wondered why.

Maybe my dreams were good, he thought to himself.

The door opened and in walked Irene. "You are up already, I see. How was your sleep?"

"It was good."

"Well, there is a shower just up the hall. I already put a towel and cloth in there for you. I will have the waiter bring you up some breakfast, then Shortman is going to be taking you shopping, okay, honey?" She nodded. "I'll see you when I return." She turned and closed the door behind.

Ice got to his feet, stretched, then walked out into the hall, and headed into the bathroom. The shower was hot and hard on his skin. It had been quite a while since he'd had a shower like this one. Afterward, he went back into the room where he saw a hot plate of grits and eggs with neatly cut halves of toast sitting on a tray. Shortman sat at the large keyboard, studying the monitors closely.

"Do you watch that thing all day and night?" he asked, taking a seat on the couch.

Shortman chuckled. "Just during business hours, but today we are closed, so I'm just looking over old footage." Ice picked over the food, indicating that he wasn't very hungry. "Are you almost ready to go? Because you don't look hungry at all."

Ice sat the tray of food on the floor and got to his feet. "I guess so."

They left the ballroom and headed out to Shortman's Lincoln Jeep. Once they were inside, Shortman turned on the radio. A popular soul song played as he pulled into the street and merged with the early morning traffic.

"So what kind of clothes do you like?" He took his eyes off the road momentarily to look at Ice.

"I like Lee jeans and stuff like that."

Shortman burst into a laugh. "Lee jeans! Nobody wears that kind of shit no more, and plus the kind of stores we are going to be shopping at don't even sell that weak-ass gear."

"Weak? What's wrong with Lee jeans?"

Shortman laughed again. "You'll understand in time." The light turned red on the corner of Blue Hill Avenue. "Shit. I always get caught at this same damn light." He slapped his palm against the steering wheel. When the light changed, he made a left turn onto Martin Luther King Boulevard. It was full of lavish clothing shops like Armani, Versace, and Homburg, among others. The strip looked like a place where only the rich and famous would shop. Shortman pulled alongside a store with a name that Ice couldn't pronounce. "Today you become Ice, Aldolphus." He smiled, turning off the vehicle.

Once inside, Ice remembered thinking that they had made a wrong turn. "What kind of a store is this?" He looked around at the suits and expensive shoes in astonishment.

"I told you: this is the place where you will start to live up to your name. You can't have a name like Ice without the threads to match."

A tall woman with coal-black hair approached. "Can I help you with anything today?" Her voice was pleasant.

"Yes, you can. I need to see your finest young men's suits and alligator shoes."

"That's so cute. Are you playing daddy today?" She smiled. Shortman returned the sentiment. "Come with me. I know just what you are looking for." They walked to the rear of the store. Ice tried on several suits before deciding on a style that he liked. Shortman picked out five pairs of alligator shoes for Ice, none costing less than two hundred greenbacks. After leaving that store, they spent a few more hours in and out of different shops purchasing watches, sweaters, and overcoats.

By the time they finished, Ice was drained. Getting back in the truck never felt so good. Ice relaxed on the passenger seat and almost instantly began to fall asleep.

"Sit back and enjoy the ride because we got a long drive to Airstead's house in Vegas. Normally we would fly, but the boss needed extra time." He laughed before pulling out into the evening traffic.

Ice looked over at Shortman. "Can you do me a favor before you take me back to Airstead's house?"

"What's on your mind, youngster?"

Ice sat up in his seat. "Before Mr. Airstead found me, I was in a hospital called Saint Joseph's, and while I was there, an old lady named Eva took care of me. She gave me this." He pulled the necklace from under his shirt, then he continued, "I had run away from Saint Joseph's for Children so that I could see her again."

"So what are you trying to ask me, kid?"

"Can you take me to see her?"

Shortman took a deep breath. He was really starting to like the kid. "Listen, Ice, I understand how you feel about the old lady, but that's all in the past. If I take you to that place, they will hold you there until the people from the shelter come back to get you, and then they going to try and lock me up for kidnapping or something worse. Can you dig it?"

"But Eva won't let that happen."

"Trust me, Ice. If the cops come, there ain't nothing little old Eva going to be able to do."

Ice knew that carrying this conversation any further would be futile. Shortman had his mind made up, and nothing was going to change it. Ice sat back in his seat and sank into a pool of once-up-on-a-time. He oddly wondered what had happened to Tank and if he would ever see him again. Then his thoughts shifted to Sofia and Clevio and the two men who murdered them in front of his very eyes on that cold night. Slowly the shadow of sleep came down and smothered his thoughts.

CHAPTER 11

AIRSTEAD DROVE HIS CAR DOWN Spotlight Boulevard in Vegas and instantly began to feel relief when he saw his eight-bedroom mansion peeking from behind the trees. Last night had been a long and dangerous one, and if it hadn't been for the young prostitute, Airstead would've been nothing but a memory of yesterday's dream.

When Spartan had arrived and told him that the explosives that had been wired to his car were done by a pro—more than likely a military guy—it bothered him; the mere thought of another soldier being as good as Spartan was troublesome. He headed up a long driveway, stopped in front of a four-car garage, then pushed a small button on his dash, and spoke into it.

"Open garage number 3." The large door began to open. After parking, he entered his home from the rear. "Lights please," he made another request before the room became bright with light. His palace had eight bedrooms, one master room, and a connecting guesthouse where Shortman resided. He walked down the hall and entered the living room. The statues of panthers and the many large plants made it resemble a very well-manicured jungle. The plush white carpet sank under his feet with each step as he began to climb the spiral staircase that had been neatly placed in the center of the room. All he could think about was sleep as he entered the bedroom, but for the sight of Irene lying stretched out on the bed, dressed in a black silk teddy that had risen above her thighs, exposing her freshly shaved honeycomb. Her hair was down and caressed her shoulders perfectly.

"I've been waiting for you, Big Daddy." Her voice was sexy and fell nicely on his ears. He smiled, loosened his tie, and began to undress. Irene got to her feet and walked gracefully up to her husband. She then took one finger and glided it across, then placed it between her legs. "You wanna taste me, don't you?" She placed her moist fingertips into his mouth.

He responded by caressing them with his tongue and absorbing her flavor. "I know what you want, girl." He walked around Irene and headed over to the disk player, then put in a CD. The sounds of Color Me Badd's "Sex You" filled the room. He turned and looked at Irene with conviction. "Dirty dance for me," he demanded, walking over and stretching out onto the mattress.

She walked to the foot of the bed and began to rotate her body to the rhythm of the music. She closed her eyes and caressed her breasts. Airstead could feel his nature rising as he removed his slacks and then his boxers, exposing the length and thickness of his erection. She smiled then placed her palm over her mound, then used her middle finger to begin pleasing herself. The band played on, and Irene didn't miss a beat. Airstead grabbed ahold of his penis, then began to stroke it slowly. The sight of her husband's massive love muscle aroused her even more. She crawled onto the bed with the grace of a panther, then snatched his hand away from his privates only to take ownership of it herself. She squeezed it until the veins were visible.

"Let me take care of this dick for you." She leaned downward, then stopped only inches away, then she puckered her full lips and blew her hot breath on his already throbbing erection. He jerked slightly from pleasure and anxiety. "Oh, you like that?" She rubbed one finger over the tip. He couldn't take anymore. He grabbed a handful of her hair, then forced her head downward.

"Suck it. Don't tease it." Irene took him into her mouth and began moving her head in an up-and-down motion. His body began to convulse with pleasure. "Oh, baby, I can feel it building," he said through clenched teeth.

She looked up at him. "You better not come until you fuck this pussy." Her voice was dominant. She turned her backside toward him. "Give it to me doggy style, Big Daddy, give to me."

He took his position behind her, then guided his rod into her honeycomb; slowly at first, to allow her moisture to loosen her tightness, then he began to pick up the speed. She began to moan and scream his name out.

"Whose pussy is this, huh? Whose is it!" he snapped as he pulled her hair with love and a splash of hate.

She began to thrust her body backward to meet each one of his powerful strokes with force. "It's yours, it's all yours, it's about to come," she cooed.

The tingling feeling entered her body, then seconds later, Airstead felt himself exploding inside her, and they both collapsed into the land of sexual paradise.

CHAPTER 12

SHORTMAN DROVE THE LENGTH OF the driveway leading to the mansion. He pushed the button on the dash and spoke into the speaker.

"Open number 3." The door lifted, and he pulled into the garage. "Wake up, Ice. We're home." He nudged the kid slightly. His eyes opened, then he sat up and stretched.

"Are we here already?"

Shortman laughed. "Already? Shit, we've been driving over four hours."

He got out of the vehicle and headed to the hatch. Ice followed. After collecting the shopping bags, they entered the mansion through the rear. You could smell the aroma of turkey in the air. "It's not Thanksgiving, but Irene must be making one of her late dinners," said Shortman.

The beauty of the home astonished the child as Shortman headed through the foyer and toward the steps. Irene stepped from the kitchen dressed in a black silk robe.

"Did you have a nice shopping trip?"

"Yes, I really did."

"I know you boys must be starved after the long day. Shortman, show him to his room and get him ready for dinner."

"No problem, queen." He chuckled before leading the way up the stairs and down a hall and into a lavishly decorated bedroom. It had a private bathroom, two walk-in closets, and a medium-sized fridge next to the king-size bed. Ice had never seen a child room like this one. "Do you like it?" Shortman studied Ice closely.

"I love it. I just never thought that I would ever have a room that looked this way."

"Well, there are a lot of things that you're gonna have that you never did before, so you might as well get used to it." He laughed, walking out of the room.

After putting his clothes away and taking a shower, Ice dressed in blue jeans and a T-shirt. As he entered the dining room, all eyes fell upon him.

"Doesn't he look handsome, Airstead?" Irene looked in her husband's direction.

Airstead looked at the boy from head to toe, then glanced at Shortman. "You did one hell of a job, Shortman, but I would like to see him in the new clothes." He laughed.

Ice took a seat at the table as Irene filled each plate with turkey and mashed potatoes. They ate in silence for a moment before Airstead spoke.

"I enrolled you at school today, so you will be starting tomorrow."

"Is it a nice school?" he asked curiously.

"I'm sure you'll like it."

The conversation went on about everything from boxing to the Latoya Jackson *Playboy* layout. After dinner, Ice helped Irene with the dishes, and they talked more, getting deeper acquainted with one another. Irene told him how they would have pool parties in the summer, and he told her about his rough life in the projects. By the time he had hit the bed that night, he had come to the conclusion that Irene was the kind of woman who he could love. She was like his mother, Sofia, in so many ways, including her resemblance. Somewhere in the child's heart, he felt a connection between himself and the woman named Irene. The thoughts brought a smile to his face as he escaped into the comforts of fairyland and dreamed of yesterday's beauty.

CHAPTER 13

THE FOLLOWING MORNING, ICE FELT butterflies in his stomach. Today was going to be his first day at his new school; he couldn't believe how much his short life had changed; there was so much confusion. On one hand, there was the innocent little boy named Aldolphus, and on the other was the wicked and coldhearted person that he was becoming, named Ice. He had no idea how to defeat the evil that had slowly begun to nest into his soul.

He showered then dressed carefully, choosing a nice Rolex watch and a casual outfit to complement it. After breakfast, Irene kissed them both, and they headed out to the garage.

"You look nervous, kid." Airstead started the car and backed out of the garage.

"No, I ain't nervous. This is just all new to me."

"Well, don't worry. The teachers and students at UNLV will treat you like a god."

"Why do you think that?" Ice looked curious.

"Because I told them you were my son, and I also make donations to their college program, so my finances help the place to operate smoothly."

"What if they find out that I'm not really your son?"

Airstead chuckled. "Don't worry about that. I got it covered just like makeup."

They turned onto a street that suddenly resembled an old farm. The tall grass and cornfields made it feel as if they had crossed over into another dimension. The early morning sun was radiant and hinting that today would be one of many good memories. After riding in silence, they turned onto UNLV Boulevard.

"There it is." Airstead pointed to the left. It was large and looked like a mini college campus. Ice looked at the large statue of the man on the horse and thought maybe he was someone important to the school. Airstead pulled his car into an empty space that said "Teachers Only," then looked over at Ice. "Are you ready, soldier?"

"I'm ready," he responded, climbing from the car.

The crowded entranceway seemed to fall silent as they entered the building. The hallway was congested with students and teachers alike. Airstead wrapped his arm around his shoulder and headed up the hall toward the office. Ice felt the burning and curious stares from a million sets of eyes as they passed. They entered the office and approached the desk.

A woman with large glasses greeted them with a gaped smile, "Hello, Mr. Gaddafi. Principal Janice is waiting for you in her office."

"Thanks, Judy." He winked at her before guiding Ice down a short hall and into another office.

Janice was like no principal Ice had seen before. She was a tall, firm, and well-built black woman; the tight-fitting red dress outlined the sculpture of her body perfectly; her high cheekbones complemented her smile; and her deep-brown eyes glared with queenly beauty.

She extended her hand. "Good morning, Mr. Gaddafi." They shook hands. "And how are you, Aldolphus?" She grabbed his hand. He couldn't help but notice her skin's softness. She took her seat, and for a moment, there was an awkward nonverbal exchange between her and Airstead. "So this is your son, huh?" She smiled.

"That's correct. My only son."

"He looks so much like you that it's unbelievable." She paused. "Well, enough idle talk. Let's get down to business." She reached into her desk and pulled out a small tablet with writing on the first page. "This is your schedule and your teachers' names. If you have any problems, feel free to walk into my office. I'm here all day." She paused. "Do you have any questions?"

"No, ma'am, I don't."

She picked up her phone. "Judy, he is ready to go." She hung up. "My secretary, Judy, is going to take you to your first class." She got to her feet as Judy entered the room.

"Ready when you are," said Judy, smiling. Ice got slowly to his feet and followed Judy.

"I will pick you up after school, okay?" Airstead embraced him. He nodded. "Okay."

As the door closed behind them, Janice walked over and locked it, then turned on her heel and faced Airstead.

"So why haven't you been returning any of my calls?" She grabbed him by the collar. "Did you forget what it was like to fuck this pussy?" She kissed his neck gently.

He chuckled. "I told you that I'm not leaving my wife. And I'm a busy man, Janice, and busy men fuck plenty of women."

"Is that a fact, Mr. Drug-Dealing Adulterer?" She reached and slowly slid down the zipper on his slacks, then grabbed his penis and began fondling him. "Well, show me how you fuck the other women, you sorry bastard."

He reacted aggressively, grabbing a handful of her hair and pulling her over to the desk, where he bent her over it, then proceeded to pull down her panties. "You wanna get fucked, huh, you fuckin' whore." He forced her head down onto the desk with one hand, then used the other to swipe the desk clean of all contents.

"I love it when you're rough with me," she cooed. He forced himself into her and not in a loving way. She moaned, "Fuck me, you sadistic motherfucker. Fuck me hard. Show me how much you hate me."

With each word, he became more aggressive in his assault. "Shut up, slut, and take this punishment like the whore you are." She met him thrust for thrust until they both climaxed with pleasure.

CHAPTER 14

AS ICE ENTERED THE CLASSROOM with Judy close behind, all eyes fell in his direction. His teacher was a bald gentleman with a full beard.

"Hello, I'm Mr. Jamison. You must be Aldolphus." They shook hands, and Judy turned and left the room. "Class, this is Aldolphus Jackson, our new student." Ice walked toward the back of the class.

A light-skinned girl with emerald-green eyes and long, curly hair caught his attention with a smile that he returned without knowing. Some of the kids giggled and whispered among themselves. His next three classes before lunch seemed to drag. When he walked into the lunchroom, he had that same feeling of a million pairs of eyes burning through him. He picked up a tray, then entered the long lunch line.

"Hi, Aldolphus." The voice came from behind and was pleasant. Ice turned, only to look into the face of the beautiful girl who had given him that lasting smile in his first class. "My name is Tracey." She gripped his hand.

"Nice to meet you, Tracey, but can you do me favor? Call me Ice. That's my nickname. Okay, cutie?"

She blushed and gave another one of those unforgettable smiles. "Okay, agreed." They both laughed.

"What you doing talking to that new guy?" The voice was harsh. Ice turned and saw that a tall blond kid had snatched Tracey by the arm and was holding her tightly.

"Get off me, Billy. You're hurting me!" she cried as tears formed in her big eyes.

Ice walked up to the taller boy calmly, then he spoke, "Let her go, Goldilocks." You could hear some laughter from the other kids, and Billy didn't take it kindly.

He glared at Ice. "I think you better back off, pretty boy," he responded through clenched teeth.

"I said let her go!" His voice was louder this time.

"Or what? Huh, punk?" Billy let go of Tracey and rolled up the sleeves of his shirt.

The cafeteria fell silent, and everyone looked on.

"Come on, chicken shit tough guy." Billy shoved Ice to get a reaction.

"I warned you, didn't I?" Ice forced a strong uppercut to the boy's midsection, folding him like an old lawn chair. He followed with two more lethal blows that brought the taller boy down like a tree struck by lightning. Teachers rushed the scene instantly but were too late. Billy was facedown with a small puddle of blood around his mouth. Ice stood over his body and glared almost in a trance at his limp body. As the school security escorted Ice to the principal's office, the nurse and her team were arriving to take Billy to the medical facility for treatment.

"What is this about?" snapped Janice, getting to her feet and looking Ice in the eye. He took a seat in the chair. "Well, I'm waiting." She drummed her fingers on the desk impatiently.

"Nothing happened," he responded flatly.

Janice slapped the desk with an open palm. "I have a bleeding student in the infirmary, and you tell me nothing happened. Look, child, this is your first day, and you're already asking for suspension. How do you think your father will react?" There was a knock at the door.

"Come in!" she yelled, running her fingers through her hair. The door opened, and in walked Judy, accompanied by Tracey.

"Miss Janice, this young lady has something she wants to tell you." Then Judy turned on her heel and closed the door behind her. Tracey walked over and took a seat next to Ice.

"This better be good, Tracey."

Tracey looked at Ice, then at Principal Janice. "It wasn't his fault. He was only trying to stop Billy from hurting me. He asked him to let go of my arm and then—"

"Say no more, Tracey." Janice interrupted, putting her hand in the air. "Is this true, Aldolphus?"

Ice nodded. "Yes, ma'am."

Janice chuckled. "It looks like the boys are a little jealous of you already. Okay, here is the deal: the next time something like this happens, please come to me because the last thing I want to do is suspend you. Now get back to class before I have a change of heart."

Ice got to his feet and hurried out of the office and down the hall.

"Wait a minute, wait a minute!" Tracey yelled from behind.

He turned and faced her. "What do you want?" His voice was harsh, and Tracey's smile turned sour.

"I just wanted to thank you for what you did for me at lunch. You didn't have to bite my head off."

Ice ran his fingers through his hair. "I'm sorry, Tracey. It's just that trouble is the last thing I need on my first day. I didn't mean to take it out on you." He leaned over and kissed her gently on the cheek. She was caught off guard and found herself blushing like never before. He turned and vanished into what seemed to Tracey like thin air.

Ice was glad when the final bell of the day sounded, indicating that school was over. He rushed down the hall and out of the exit doors as quickly as possible. He was pleased to see Airstead seated in the car, waiting for him.

"Hey, Ice! Ice!" called a familiar voice. He turned and saw Tracey making her way through the crowd. "I have something for you." She reached into her bag as she approached and handed him a small folded paper. "That's my phone number. Call me." She turned and raced toward a yellow bus that was waiting there. Ice walked over and joined Airstead in the car.

"I see that your first day was a success."

Ice laughed. "It was okay." He thought about telling Airstead about what happened with Billy but decided against it.

"I have some business to take care of in LA with my contractors. The private jet is gassed up and ready to go. Do you want to join me or hang at home with Irene?"

"I guess I will go with you. I'm interested in learning more about your business."

The child's words surprised Airstead. "I see you're starting to feel comfortable with your new family."

"Is there any reason that I shouldn't? I mean, you and my dad were best friends in school, right?"

Airstead smiled. "That's correct, baby boy."

After the short flight, Airstead picked up his rental car and headed to Rusty's. As he pulled into the parking lot across the street from where Rusty's once stood, he smiled to himself. The empire was just a construction job away from being his. They climbed from the car and approached four men in hard hats talking among themselves. A tall man with a stocky build looked up from his conversation.

"Hey, Mr. Gaddafi, glad you could make it on such a short notice."

"What's up, Buddy?" They shook hands.

"So whatcha got for me?" Buddy asked.

Airstead reached into his blazer and pulled out a small roll of paper. "These are the blueprints. Look them over and tell me what you think." He folded his arms across his chest and studied Buddy closely as the man began to examine the blueprints. Ice stood quietly, observing both Airstead's and Buddy's silence.

Suddenly he looked up from the paperwork. "This place is going to be a fucking tourist attraction. There's not a casino that would ever be able to compare to this one except the Vegas ones."

Airstead laughed at Buddy's sentiment. "That's why we are building in LA, the big City of Dreams. And besides, how many Vegas casinos have three different nightclubs, a simulated beach area, and a lottery?"

"None that I know of," Buddy responded.

"So there you have it: Gaddafi's Palace reigning supreme." He raised his hands as if he could see a vision. They talked a little while longer about details, then Airstead and Ice headed back to the vehicle.

"We have another stop to make before heading home. And oh yeah, in case you think I didn't hear about your little scuffle today at school, I did."

Ice felt his heart sink. "How did you find out?"

"Don't worry yourself with that. As long as you didn't get beat up, I don't care. You need to learn to be almost heartless in this world. Always remember that, son." They drove a few moments in silence before Airstead pulled in the front of a two-story home in a nice middle-class neighborhood. "Wait here." He exited the car, leaving it running.

Ice relaxed in his seat and closed his eyes. Airstead walked onto the porch and knocked lightly. The sun was just setting, giving the street a gloomy blue color. The door was opened by a very attractive black woman, maybe thirty years of age. Airstead forced his way into the house, knocking the woman to the floor.

"Where the fuck is Little Jimmy?" He gripped her shirt and snatched the small woman to her feet.

"I don't know. I swear I don't. I haven't seen him for days."

He shoved her onto the couch, then pulled the .357 smoke pole from his jacket. "You know what, Linda. I've been more than patient with you and your punk-ass husband. I gave you a place to live, put clothes on your backs, and all I asked for y'all to do was move a few lousy kilos of White Girl for me. So here we are seven months in, and I haven't seen one greenback yet. I think that I have had enough of this game." He cocked back the hammer on his gun, then took aim. "Now you got five minutes to tell me where that bitch is hiding with my cash." His threat went over well, for it didn't take long at all before she started to sing.

"Okay, okay, okay, he is at my sister's place down the street," she blurted.

Airstead laughed. "Good, now I know you have a key stashed around here somewhere." His expression was intense.

"I don't but she has one in the flowerpot on her porch. Just please don't kill me. I will do anything that you want."

He laughed. "Anything I want, huh? You know what, Linda. Just talking to you makes my dick hard, so why don't you suck it off."

He stepped closer to her, then unzipped his pants. She reached for his privates with trembling hands; the tears were galloping steady down her cheeks. He put the pistol to her head. "Now I'm going to give you five minutes to make me come. If you take a minute longer then you're one dead bitch." He looked at his Rolex. She took him into her mouth slowly at first, closing her eyes to fight back the constant flow of tears that drenched her face. "Come on, bitch. The clock's off snooze." He forced the barrel deeper into her cheek. She began to move faster, twisting her head from one side to the other. "Oh yeah, baby, oh yeah, suck it deep. Deep throat that meat." She began to work harder, and in minutes, his climax built up and erupted into her mouth. She continued to take him in until his penis went limp. She wiped her lips, then looked up at him.

"How did I do?"

He looked at his watch with a devilish smirk. "Three minutes and twenty seconds." He zipped his pants.

Linda gazed at him as if she were waiting for more instruction. "What the fuck are you looking at, you dirty bitch? You disgust me. Cover your face. I don't want to see it!"

She placed both of her palms over her face and began to sob. Her silent prayer began with "Dear God," but I don't believe that he was listening.

Airstead lifted his weapon, slowly took aim, and fired two shots. The echo brought Ice back to reality, and his heart thumped like tribal drums. Airstead walked calmly out of the house, jumped behind the wheel, and peeled out into the street.

Ice looked over at him. "What happened in there?"

"Nothing to worry about, son." He parked the car across the street from a duplex. "Wait here." He climbed from the car and headed up the steps to the house. Ice sat back in his seat and oddly wondered what was taking shape. The strangest thing about his thoughts was the diabolical voice that told him to follow Airstead into the house and participate in anything that took place, but he quickly decided against it.

Airstead felt around in the flowerpot until he found the key. He inserted it into the lock as quietly as possible, then pushed the door open. He could hear the muffled sound of moans and the rocking bed against the ceiling. He looked upward, then smirked, shutting the door ever so carefully before taking out his weapon and heading up the stairs. One of them creaked loudly, causing him to pause and make sure that his prey was still unaware. The screams of intimacy continued as he headed down the dark hall. He stood outside the door briefly before turning the knob and opening it. The one called Little Jimmy was not so little at all; in fact, he was well over six feet and three hundred plus pounds, and he was driving himself in and out of the smaller woman who lay under him. She cooed and moaned his name in a sequence that only could be described as rehearsed. She opened her eyes and fixed on the figure standing in the door pointing a gun at the fat backside of Jimmy. Her shock was so intense that all she could do was lightly nudge Jimmy, who was still occupied with cherishing her body.

"I wish I had a video camera because this is without question going to be a moment to remember."

The sound of Airstead's voice caused Jimmy to roll off the woman. Fear and death were written in his eyes like the writing on the wall. The girl covered her naked body.

Little Jimmy put his hands up. "I have your money, Airstead. I was going to call you later to meet up. Ain't that right, Candy?" His voice trembled as he looked over at the girl for her to cosign his bullshit.

"That's right. That was the plan." Her response was clumsy to say the least.

Airstead laughed. "You know what, Jimmy. You're a sorry son of a bitch. You leave your wife and tell her that you're going to hide out with my money, and then I come down here and what do I see but your black ass humping up and down on your sister-in-law. Now what do you think Linda would think about that?" He lowered his smoke pole momentarily.

"Come on, Airstead. I have your money." Little Jimmy got to his feet.

"Don't take another step, you fat rodent." He turned and took aim at Candy. "You get up and get the money." She got to her feet, letting the blanket drop to the floor, showing every curve on her naked body. As she walked past Airstead toward the closet, he slapped her bottom with authority, then looked at Jimmy. "Is that pussy any good?" Jimmy didn't respond. Airstead watched her closely as she returned from the closet, carrying a leather backpack. He snatched it from her grasp. "Now go over there and stand next to Little Dick Jimmy." He chuckled at his own joke. He knelt then opened the bag. Among the contents were a loaded Desert Eagle and several stacks of money. "Looks like you were expecting me, Little Dick. Too bad I got the drop on you, or I might have been minced meat from the power of this weapon." He got to his feet, then tucked the cannon into his waistline.

"Now it's time to play a little game." He walked up to Jimmy and grabbed him by the neck and forced him backward. Then he snatched Candy by the hair. "Get on your knees." He forced her to the ground in front of Jimmy.

She began to sob, "Please don't kill me. Please don't. I will do whatever you want."

"Never mind that. Your sister already took care of my load." He laughed. "But don't worry, beautiful. I'm not going to kill you. Jimmy will." The overweight man had a look of both fear and confusion in his eyes. Airstead walked and stood behind Jimmy, then leaned close to his ear and began to whisper, "Now listen here, Little Dick. I'm going to put this gun in your hand, then I want you to pull the trigger." He placed the gun into Jimmy's trembling hands, then covered them with his own as not to relinquish control of the weapon. He looked at Candy. "Now open your beautiful mouth." He aimed the weapon at her face. Her pleas for mercy became louder, then she closed her eyes. "Open it, bitch," he snapped, squeezing Jimmy's hand tighter around the gun. She opened her mouth slowly, all the while trying to stop the chatter of her teeth. "Now pull the fucking trigger. Pull it now!" Jimmy's trembling finger touched the trigger. The blast was loud, and the heated hollow point entered her mouth and exited through the back of her neck, causing blood spatter to hit the wall. Her lifeless body hit the wooden floor. Jimmy's hands trembled, and his face was covered in a nervous sweat. "Now you see how easy that was. Not hard at all." He took the weapon from Jimmy. "Now don't turn around until I'm gone, okay, Little Dick?" He laughed. Slowly, he lifted his smoke pole and aimed it at the back of Jimmy's head.

Ice was becoming worried; he had heard the first shot, and when Airstead didn't appear, his heart began to race. Then suddenly there was another shot. He opened the car door and landed one foot on the ground. Out of the mist, Airstead appeared, wearing a bright smile and walking calmly down the steps. "No need to come looking for me, baby boy." He got into the car, then peeled out onto the lonely, dark street.

Killing was a way of life for this ruthless man known as Airstead Gaddafi. Once upon a time, Ice would've been afraid of a beast like him, but deep within his heart, there was an overwhelming desire to love and protect this diabolical walking time bomb that could explode on contact.

CHAPTER 15

"WHAT ARE YOU THINKING ABOUT, son?" Airstead broke the silence.

"Nothing much," his response was flat.

"You're lying to me, son." The light turned red then green; they drove farther, then turned onto a suburban street called Beacon Hill. "Well, son, what's bothering you? I've never heard you this quiet before."

Ice took a deep breath. "It's not really bothering me. I just want to know more about what happened back there." He looked at Airstead intently.

Airstead smirked. "Just put it this way: whatever you saw happening in your mind is what happened in my reality." He parked outside a large beautiful white house. Ice repeated Airstead's words over in his head and tried to gather an accurate understanding of the short riddle. "Are you coming with me, or are you going to sit in the car and daydream all night?" Ice smiled then got out of the car and followed Airstead up the pink-painted concrete steps. He pulled a set of keys from his pocket, then opened the door.

The sound of muffled music could be heard coming from a closed door off to the left. He walked up and knocked gently. Moments passed and voices could be heard. Then the door opened. Behind it was a short Spanish woman with a gorgeous figure, tanned skin, and silky long, black hair. Her lips were outlined with a gloss, and the tiny miniskirt fit her perfectly.

"Hey, Daddy." She grabbed him up in the collar and pulled him into the room.

"What's up, Kaila," he responded. Ice lets his eyes travel the room. It was full of women walking around in thongs. Shortman was seated on a couch between a blond girl and a dark-skinned sista; he got to his feet, and as Airstead approached, they slapped hands.

"How did things go at Jimmy's?"

"Things got a little dirty on the Westside, but my girlfriend managed to have things her way," he said as he touched the bulge under his coat.

Ice looked on as Kaila and a short white girl danced together. He couldn't believe his eyes when they began to feverishly kiss one another in the mouth.

"So where's the cash?" Airstead asked, looking down at Shortman.

"I'll get it." Shortman headed toward a connecting room.

Kaila walked over to Airstead. "When can I get some of this?" She grabbed his crotch; he pushed her hand away.

"Do you see that little boy over there?" He pointed to Aldolphus. She looked at the boy and gave a smile before gliding her tongue over her perfect lips.

"Yeah, I see him."

"Well, that's my son, and he is about to turn thirteen. Why don't you take him in the back and toss the pussy up for him. He needs a little hair on his balls." She turned on her heel and walked over to Ice. Airstead smiled as they vanished into the back room.

Shortman appeared carrying a brown paper bag. "Here it is, boss: one hundred thousand big ones counted and stacked."

Airstead took the bag. "Good job, Shortman. I don't know how I could survive without you."

"Hey, man, my loyalty is with this family to the end. Hey, where did Ice get to?" He looked around the room.

Airstead laughed. "I sent him in the back with Madame Kaila to get his first shot of a snapping pussy."

They both laughed hard. "I don't know, boss. She might drive your little son crazy."

"I doubt it. The kid's a tiger, and plus he has moxie."

"Now just relax." Kaila knelt before Ice. "Now I'm going to suck your dick and make you love me." Her words made his heart flutter, and the butterflies fought with one another in his stomach. She unzipped his pants, reached into his shorts, and revealed his small penis. She smiled, then rubbed one finger over it. "Ooo, this dick is cute. Make it hard for Mama so I can see how big it gets." The way the words flowed from her lips with the strong accent caused his nature to almost immediately rise. She smiled. "That's the way I like it," she cooed as he became erect in her palms. She then opened her mouth and covered him whole. He began to sweat, and his legs quivered from pleasure. She kissed it gently, then got to her feet. "Follow me." She walked over to the bed. "Lie down, baby boy." She pushed him onto the bed. His small penis stayed at attention and throbbed for her. She removed her blouse, then took off her underwear but left the mini on, then she crawled onto the bed and straddled his small body. "Close your eyes, baby, and enjoy the ride." She used two fingers to shut his lids and then she mounted him. He felt the warm wetness of her sugar walls and instantly became intoxicated with pleasure.

"Man, it ain't nothing like watching a gang of hookers get it on," said Shortman, looking at Airstead.

"You got that right, Shorty, and you know what? I think I'm ready to join in and have some fun." He got to his feet and began to undress. There were six women lying in a circle, each one performing oral sex on the other. He knelt next to the Asian girl, then snatched her from between the legs of a redhead, freckled-face woman. "Let me taste her pussy." He feverishly kissed her in the mouth. The other girl got to her knees and took him into her mouth. Shortman approached from behind, then eased himself into her flesh. She let out a moan and then began to perform better than before. The scene was out of an X-rated video; the beastly and carefree behavior of these humans went on for hours, then eventually ended in a sweaty climax.

CHAPTER 16

AS THE DAYS PASSED, ICE somewhat began to forget the scary demons of his brutal past life. With Airstead, life had become one big adventure: you never knew what to expect from him; he was truly an unpredictable and diabolical individual.

Ice wondered often about Eva and prayed that God was taking care of her. Tank was also in the front of his thoughts, and in his solitude, he would repeat their secret bond. On the day he turned thirteen, he exited the school, accompanied by his new girlfriend, Tracey Spencer. He smiled as he saw Airstead waiting for him.

"There is my dad." He jogged over to the car with Tracey close behind.

"You look like you're feeling lucky today, young buck." He smiled at Ice.

"He thinks he's getting old." Tracey cosigned with a smile.

"Girl, be quiet." He wrapped his arm around her.

"You two love birds better take it easy. I ain't gonna pay for a wedding until you both graduate." Airstead laughed, getting into the car and starting it.

Tracey looked at Ice. "Call me later, okay?"

"I will, babe."

"Promise me, Ice." She gave a cute smile.

He leaned forward and gently kissed her lips. "I promise, baby." He turned on his heel and got into the car. Tracey smiled as she watched the car pull away.

They drove in silence for several moments. "I have a special birthday present for you."

Ice studied Airstead's profile closely; it was something about the way the words had come out, along with the blank expression worn on his usually radiant face, that hinted at some sort of mysterious story.

"What is it? A new Rolex?"

Airstead chuckled. "Now if I tell you, son, then it wouldn't be a surprise, would it?" His face was still a solid mask of gloom. He drove onto a hilly road that was empty and quiet like a scene from *The Twilight Zone*.

Airstead looked ahead without blinking an eye, and Ice oddly wondered what was traveling through his unpredictable mind. He turned onto a dirt road and drove until an old dilapidated cabin appeared. He parked in the rear and turned off the engine.

"What's this place?" His question was filled with curiosity. Airstead glared at him, and Ice could not recall a time that this man had given him this sort of look.

"It's going to be the place where you celebrate your best birthday." He got out of the car, then headed down a path toward the cabin. As they approached the door, Airstead turned and looked him in the eye. Ice noticed a hint of water building behind his lids, which would be unusual for someone with ice in his veins.

He opened the door and stepped in. Ice felt a shiver as he took in the condition of the cabin. Cobwebs were everywhere, and the windows had all been broken; shards of glass could be heard cracking under their shoes as they walked. Airstead led the way into a connecting room. "Happy birthday, son."

The sight before Ice resurrected a dark, gloomy nightmare that buried itself as a secret cemetery in his heart. He was eleven years old the last time he had looked into those deep, piercing eyes belonging to the demon named Sonny. Both of his parents' slayers were tied and gagged and strapped to chairs. He could read the fear in their eyes, and this gave him a rush of pleasure. He looked up at Airstead.

"Happy birthday, son. There is no justice like your justice." He placed a small-caliber handgun into his hand. His heart began to race, and the adrenaline rushed to his fingertips. "Lay those bastards to rest, Ice. Do you remember what they did to Sofia?" No sooner were the words spoken, the memory came crashing down in a sudden storm.

*   *   *   *   *

Flashback

Aldolphus crept slowly down the steps, taking a seat on the fourth one, then he peeked around the wall into the living room. His heart sank into a black abyss. Sofia was naked and tied to a chair; her face and body were covered in bloody gashes. A large man with a bullwhip with what looked like razors attached, stood over her. He wore dark sunglasses and a white Stetson hat. The other man was shorter, stocky with curly hair; he had a chubby face and spoke in a deep Italian accent.

"You've been telling me that same thing for two months now." He glared at Clevio.

"I know, Sonny. Just give me another week." The tears ran down Ice's face. Sonny chuckled then looked at the man with the whip and gave a nod. He raised the whip, then swung it violently across Sofia's bare breast; blood flowed out of her body and raced down her stomach.

*   *   *   *   *

Airstead's voice brought Ice back to reality. "Turn those bastards into ghosts," he whispered. Ice felt the tears run down his cheek. He raised the pistol slowly and aimed it at Sonny.

"My nightmare is over." He pulled the trigger; the blast echoed, and the bullet cut the air like a razor and hit Sonny in the forehead. His head fell limp to his chest and smoke escaped from the wound. Ice quickly took aim at the other figure. His expression was cold and blank as he pulled the trigger three more times, each bullet hitting him in the chest and leaving him lifeless.

Justice had an evil way of catching up to those who dwell in the shadows of hell.

The nightmare had come to an end. But this was the birth date of another heartless ghetto soldier.

BOOK 2

Loyalty Turned Lethal

CHAPTER 1

ICE WOKE UP IN HIS bed with the buzzing of his alarm clock. Five years had passed, and he was now eighteen years of age and ready to graduate high school. He ran his fingers through his thick curls and lifted his 6-foot, 195-pound frame from the bed, walked to the bathroom, and looked at himself in the mirror.

People weren't being untruthful when they told him that he and Airstead were twins; they had the same curly hair and the clear, ice-cold blue eyes. As the old saying goes, "The longer you're around someone, the more you become to look alike." He laughed at his thoughts, then gripped his necklace tightly.

"I wonder what Eva would say if she could see me now," he spoke just above a whisper.

He got into the shower; the hot water warmed him, and thoughts of Tracey and their wild sex life brought a smile to his face. In his own way, he loved Tracey; she had been his sweetheart since middle school. But now they were both young adults; things had a strange way of changing after high school; people developed their own minds and desires. But Tracey was the sort of girl who would stand behind him even when she knew that he was wrong.

He first realized her loyalty when she had discovered that he had developed a liking for snorting cocaine. She was upset and told him that she didn't condone his drug of choice but would do whatever to help him dispose of his habit. Weeks later, he had told her that he quit just to keep her quiet, but he vowed to never use the drug around her again.

Airstead never seemed to have a problem with it. In fact, Ice and his father had snorted a few lines together. They celebrated the opening of Gaddafi's Palace, which had now become the most popular gambling spot in LA. Airstead had closed down the BBC Ballroom a year after the casino had opened.

Ice turned off the water, grabbed a towel, then dried himself. He slipped on his bathrobe and slippers, then headed into the bedroom where he found Shortman standing with a big smile.

"What's up, baby boy? Are you ready for your big day?"

Ice took a breath before responding, "I guess so, but right now I need a pickup."

Shortman laughed. "Say no more, my man. I came prepared for this party." He reached into his jacket pocket and came out with a small bag filled with a white powder. He dumped some of it onto the back of Ice's hand.

"It's a white Christmas," he said, before snorting up the powder. Shortman laughed then headed toward the door.

"Airstead wants to see you as soon as you're dressed, okay?"

"All right. Tell him that I will be down in a minute." He dressed in a black Versace suit and a white crewneck shirt, and the topping was the white Homburg hat with the black strap.

He walked into the kitchen and kissed Irene on the cheek as she prepared breakfast at the stove. She smiled and hugged him closely. "You look so handsome today, baby. I know your mother would be so proud of you."

He caressed Irene's face between his palms. "Listen, Irene, that nightmare is over. Just let it die, okay?" He kissed her forehead.

"Today is your big day, son." Airstead walked into the kitchen. The years hadn't changed him much; minus the salt-and-pepper hair, he looked the same. His walk was still strong, and he could trade body punches with the best of them; the late forties had been treating him well. After breakfast, Irene went up to get dressed.

"Come with me. I have something to show you," said Airstead, getting up from the table and heading toward the front door. Ice and Shortman followed close behind. As they walked onto the porch, the sun was just peeking from behind the dark clouds. They headed over to the garage.

"Open door number 1." The door opened slowly and eventually revealed a black Mercedes-Benz convertible with deep-dish rims and fully loaded. Ice allowed a smile to appear on his face.

"It's yours, son." Airstead tossed the keys at Ice.

Shortman smiled. "Ain't she a beauty?" he whispered to himself.

Ice turned and looked at Airstead. "I love you, Dad," he said as he pulled Airstead close to him.

"I love you, too, son."

Airstead and Irene drove in one car while Ice and Shortman tested out the new Benz.

"Do you want another pickup?" Shortman dangled the bag of powder before Ice.

"Yeah, give me another one." He turned his palm over, then snorted the powder quickly.

"So whatcha gonna do now that this high school shit is over?" Shortman looked at Ice.

There was a pause, then Ice smiled. "I'm going to live a gangster's dream and a player's fantasy until the day that I'm sleeping with the worms."

Shortman laughed. "You ain't ready for that life yet. You still pussy whipped over Tracey."

"Man, whatever. I'm telling you, Shorty. I run that girl. Whatever I say goes."

"Shit, I can't tell yet. Whenever she calls, your ass goes running. She probably be chaining you up and spanking your light-ass red." He laughed harder.

"Shut up, Shorty. You're that same little midget from that movie *Penitentiary* that was running around raping motherfuckers. I'm going to start calling you the Midnight Thug."

They joked the rest of the ride until they reached the lot of the school where students and parents mingled among one another. As Ice got out of the vehicle, he could see Tracey approaching. She was more beautiful than he remembered her. Her hair was long and curly, and she was shaped like an hourglass.

"Hey, honey." She hugged him and kissed his lips. "Like your new car." She drank in the beauty of the vehicle.

"Hey, we will see you guys at the ceremony," yelled Airstead, heading into the building with Irene. Shortman started behind the couple before turning on his heel and facing Tracey.

"Hey, Tracey, don't beat him too bad tonight." He laughed.

"I'll try to take it easy on him." She winked.

"So I guess today is the day, huh." Ice changed the subject.

She smiled. "Today is our day, honey, and we will have plenty more as long as you keep loving me the way you do." She kissed him with passion, exploring his mouth with her tongue. "I love you with all that I am, Aldolphus Jackson." He caressed her body in his muscular arms, then kissed her forehead.

"I will always love you, Tracey."

The ceremony lasted about two hours. The band played a few songs, and one of the students told twenty minutes of jokes. After the closing, which was given by the principal, everyone was dismissed. Ice was overwhelmed with joy. It was finally over. After four years of high school, he was now preparing himself to become a respected and well-known business tycoon. A little bloodshed might be involved, but who cares; he had long ago learned how to pull a trigger.

He walked to his car and smiled to himself. Tracey approached with two of her friends at her side.

"Hey, baby, I have the keys to my grandmom's house, and we're having a party there in about an hour. Are you coming?" She dangled the keys.

He smiled. "I'll be there. Just let me go and change my clothes."

"Well, don't keep me waiting too long, Big Daddy. Your poom poom might get lonely." She winked and her girlfriends giggled. He chuckled and watched her buttocks earthquake under her gown as she walked.

"Don't stare too long, boy, or you might catch a charge for reckless eyeballing." Airstead laughed, appearing at his side.

Ice gave a smile. "Hey, where's Shorty and Irene?"

"They went home already. I thought you and I would go somewhere and have a serious talk."

Ice frowned. "A talk about what?"

"About life after death," Airstead responded, jumping into the passenger side of the car.

Ice got in the car, started it, then pulled out of the school parking lot and onto the street. Airstead almost immediately began to bark out directions, calling out left and right turns almost unexpectedly. They drove onto a dirt road that was surrounded by uninhabited open land.

"Stop here!" he yelled as they arrived at a large field. Ice stopped the vehicle and observed that the wide-open land appeared to have no ending.

"Where in the hell are we?"

"It's paradise, son."

He got out of the car and took a seat on the hood. Ice followed and took a seat next to him. The weather was nice and breezy and caressed the grass beautifully. Airstead looked straight ahead, wearing a solid mask of gloom. The air was empty of voices, and neither person dared to break it for what seemed like an eternity. The wind whistled, and the sun hid behind some clouds momentarily.

"So where do you go from here, son?"

"What do you mean, where do I go from here?" He chuckled.

Airstead took a deep breath; his expression impatient. "I mean, now that school is over. What do you plan on doing with your life?"

"Well, I want to become deeper involved in the family business."

Airstead laughed at his response. "Do you know what it takes to become deeper involved in this business?" He raised his voice. "You gotta be ready to die. Are you ready to die? Huh, Ice? Huh, are you?" He got up and stood directly in front of Ice. Ice glared back at Airstead but opted to remain silent. "Okay, you choose not to answer me, then I'll have to make you." He reached into his jacket and pulled out his .45 caliber semiautomatic and put it to the boy's face. "You scared now, ain't you, boy? Are you ready to die now? Huh, punk?" Ice looked into the black hole of the weapon that was being pointed at him. Then he slowly pushed himself from the hood of the car.

"The one thing that I have learned to live with since I was eleven was death. If you really believe that I'm afraid of death, then pull the damn trigger." Airstead gave a devilish smile, then cocked the hammer slowly. Suddenly Ice slapped the barrel of the weapon, knocking it to the ground and causing it to let off a round. Airstead swung a left hook, catching Ice in the jaw and instantly knocking him onto the hood of the car. The blow stunned him momentarily. He shook it off, then jumped to his feet. Airstead's right cross was already incoming. Ice ducked and in one motion scooped Airstead up from the ground and body-slammed him ruthlessly onto the car, making a huge dent. Airstead retaliated with several powerful upper-cuts; then he stuffed his knee into the boy's midsection, knocking him to the ground. Then he lunged at him. Ice kicked both feet into his chest, knocking him back onto the car yet again. He recovered from the ground quickly, then tossed a right that caught Airstead in the mouth. He followed up with a body shot that put the older gang-ster on his knees. Blood appeared on both of their faces. Airstead next took a cheap shot, striking Ice in the groin and bringing him to his knees so that they were face-to-face; then he gripped his face between his palms and gave the boy a vicious headbutt that made him dizzy. Airstead got to his feet and looked down on Ice. His breathing was heavy.

"You done yet, boy?"

Ice got up, moving lethargically; then like lightning, he exploded, throwing a machine gun of uppercuts that folded Airstead up like a big bag. Then he gripped him by the back of his pants and tossed him headfirst into the dirt. Airstead looked dazed and confused from the fusillade of punches that he had absorbed. Ice then walked over and picked up the pistol from the ground and stood over Airstead. He knelt next to him, then gripped him up in the collar and put the smoke pole to his head.

"Now who's the punk? Are you ready to die? I said are you ready to die?" A tear escaped from his eye. He had grown to love this man; the one person that he could trust with his life. He realized that kill-ing him would be next to impossible.

Airstead laughed. "I'm proud of you, boy. I'm real damn proud of you," he whispered.

Ice let go of his shirt, then dropped the gun to the ground. He walked to his car, got behind the wheel, then took one last look at Airstead before making a sharp U-turn that formed clouds of smoke, then disappeared into the mist. Airstead got to his feet, then smiled to himself. He knew within his heart of hearts that the child that he had groomed into a young man was ready to play the game, and only by the blood rules.

CHAPTER 2

ANGRY AND FRUSTRATED, ICE SPED up the driveway to Tracey's house. He shifted the gear aggressively into park, then leaped from the car. Still bloody and dirty from the fight, he headed to the front door. Music could be heard coming from the other side. He rang the doorbell and waited. No answer; he rang again. Still no answer. He turned on his heel and walked around to the back of the house. The yard was crowded with people. Ice scanned the crowd and spotted Tracey seated at a table near the swimming pool, laughing and joking with her friends. As he approached, the conversation and laughter had a cardiac arrest and died instantly. Tracey looked up at him.

"Oh god, what happened to you, babe?" she exclaimed, getting to her feet and caressing his bruised face. "Come on. Let's go inside."

Her friends whispered and talked among themselves as they walked away and through the glass doors leading into the house. Tracey walked over to the sink and ran some water onto a cloth and began aiding her wounded boyfriend. You could see the tears that she fought back forming in her eyes.

"What happened, Ice?" Her voice was gentle and filled with compassion.

"I had a fistfight with my father."

Tracey's look was one of astonishment. "What about? Your father has never hit you."

Ice took a deep breath. "It's a long story, and I'm not really up to explaining."

She wiped his face clean of blood, then caressed it. "I understand, honey. I just want you to know that I'm here for you if you need me." She kissed him gently.

"I need to lie down. My body needs a rest," he said, sluggishly.

Tracey gave a sympathetic smile. "Go upstairs and take the room on the right. I will make you something to drink, then come up and keep you company."

Ice turned and left the room, then suddenly turned and peeked his head back into the room. "One more thing: call Irene or Shortman and tell them that I left Airstead in a field near the school. I'm sure one of them knows where I'm talking about."

"Okay, I will take care of everything, baby. You just go upstairs and relax." He walked up the stairs and into the bedroom; his thoughts confusing as well as painful.

"Why would Airstead want to hurt me?" he questioned himself. It was a test; it had to be. he concluded. Tracey entered the room carrying a small tray with a glass of lemonade on it. He sat up and took it, then swallowed it within seconds.

She smiled. "If I had known you were that thirsty, I would have brought you a whole pitcher." She laughed, taking the glass and setting it on the tray next to the bed. He reclined back and placed both hands behind his head and stared blankly up at the ceiling. She sat next to him and began rubbing her fingers through his hair. "Everything is going to be okay. I promise you that," she whispered. He grabbed her hand and kissed it. She smiled. "Just lie there and let me make love to you."

She pulled his shirt over his head and began running her manicured fingers over his hairy chest and teasing his nipples until he quivered with excitement. His response to her only increased the energy. She unbuckled his pants and released the throbbing muscle that was fighting to get free. She could feel her clitoris twitching as she performed oral ecstasy on the man she loved. His body relaxed under her sexual spell, and the desire between them increased so much that Tracey lifted her dress, pulled her panties aside, and mounted him, tossing her head back in pleasure all the while. He grabbed her waist aggressively, but she quickly slapped his hands away. "I told you to let me make love to you, didn't I? Didn't I?" She raised her voice slightly, then began to work her hips in a circular motion. He gripped the sheets tightly. "Tell me when you're coming, tell me, baby," she cooed between breaths. He could feel the eruption building like the strongest volcano.

"It's coming, baby, its coming." She leaned forward and kissed him feverishly, then lifted her body so that only the head of his penis was left inside her. She then contracted her pink panther muscles around him and began to work at a faster pace.

"This is your pussy. It's all yours, baby." She could feel his hot come filling up her walls, and his orgasm set off a chain of events in her body, causing her to convulse, then collapse onto his chest. The breathing of them both was heavy, and the only sound in the universe.

He ran his fingers through her hair "I love you, Tracey," he whispered.

She had never in her young life felt so safe. "I love you too." Something in her tone sounded odd and untypical. He adjusted his head and looked her in the eye and noticed they were full of tears.

"What's wrong, baby?" his question was full of curiosity.

"I heard a really bad rumor about you, and I want you to tell me the truth."

He studied her closely. "Someone told me that you were skipping college and going into your family's business with your father. Is that the truth?"

He sat up. "Who told you that?"

"It doesn't matter who told me. I just want to know if it's true," she cried.

He took a deep breath, then fanned his fingers through his hair. "Yes, it's true. Are you happy now?"

"No, I'm not fucking happy! What about us, Ice? What about our love?" She got to her feet, tears running like a river.

"Look, Tracey, calm down. It's not the end of the world. We can still be together."

"How can you say that? I'll be way in fuckin' New York City while you run around Vegas doing god-knows-what. I refuse to be pulling out my hair and busting my brains wondering what you're doing."

He jumped to his feet. "Is that what this is about? You knowing what I'm doing while you're away? I thought you trusted me."

She tossed her hands as if she had heard enough. "Okay, Ice, just leave. Please leave now!" she snapped.

"Tracey, you don't mean that."

"Yes, I do, and don't tell me what I mean. Now get out!" she yelled.

He quickly dressed, slid on his shoes, then headed toward the door. He stopped before making his exit, and without turning to face her, he said, "If you ever need me, don't hesitate to call. I love you, Tracey." He closed door behind.

Overwhelmed with emotion, Tracey picked the glass up from the nightstand and whirled it at the door, shattering it to pieces. She covered her face and sobbed loudly. Ice got into his car and started the engine.

Love has a funny way of holding captive the ones that understand it; the thorns of a first love burn like a hellfire but die under a single teardrop of water.

CHAPTER 3

GADDAFI'S PALACE WAS IN FULL swing as Ice walked through the doors. He walked past the gambling stations and headed into the adjoining nightclub. The dance floor was packed, and the booths were congested. He took a seat in the back corner alone. The loud music vibrated and filled his head.

"Hey, sexy man." The voice woke him from his trance. It was Kaila. She had since traded in her hooker boots to become a waitress. Ice looked up into her still beautiful face and gave a smirk.

"I don't feel that sexy, that's for sure."

"Hold that thought." Kaila turned and yelled to the Asian waitress passing by, "May Ling, May Ling, bring two rum and Cokes over when you get the chance," then slid into the booth next to him.

"Now tell me why you're looking so sad, honey."

"Just female problems: nothing I can't handle."

Kaila looked perplexed. "Don't tell me that pretty little young girl you had then up and left you."

He chuckled. "No, it ain't nothing like that. She just doesn't trust me, and it's been a month since we talked last."

"Well, I wouldn't trust you either, as fine as you are." She laughed. May Ling brought the drinks and put them on the table.

Ice took a sip. "Oh yeah, well you trusted me enough to give that pussy when I was a young buck though." He laughed and she laughed harder.

"Oh, please, you was just a little dick baby boy when I sat on that thing."

"That's true, and now you're talking like you're ready for a rematch or something."

"Don't tempt me, Ice. I heard you got a horse dick down there, and besides, I have always wanted to fuck in a crowded club."

He laughed. "So why don't you jump on it and find out?"

Kaila looked around to see if anyone was watching before she removed her panties from under her skirt. "Let's see if you got what it takes." She straddled him. "I'm so curious about the legend of the big dick." She caressed his crotch, and her eyes grew big in astonishment. "Oh my god. It is true."

He forced himself in her with an aggression that made her let out a moan of pain and pleasure. "I'm going to make you love me, remember that, huh?" He stroked her harder. The music only made the moment more intense and muffled their terms of endearment and then without warning, they arrived separate but came together. Kaila took a deep breath.

"That young girl would be a damn fool to let you go." She got to her feet and pulled her skirt back down.

He smiled. "Come back for thirds if you think you're ready."

She waived. "I think I'm getting too old to handle y'all young boys, and especially the ones with nine-inch dicks."

Shortman approached. "What's up, little brother?" He took a seat. "Damn, I smell catfish in the worst way. Did the menu change?" He looked at Kaila.

"Fuck you, short dick." She grabbed her drink, then walked away.

"So you fucked her for old time's sake, huh?"

Ice chuckled. "That's the way it goes when you get stressed out and your girl closes the hole up on you."

"I can dig it. Do you need a pickup?" He reached into his jacket and placed the silver case onto the table. Ice opened it, removed his straw from his drink, and began making small lines with the powder. Afterward, he used the straw as a vacuum and snorted two lines, then passed it to Shortman, and he did the same. "So when is Tracey leaving for school?"

"I'm not absolutely sure. I've been calling her for the last month, and all she does is hang up on me. Her right-hand girl told me that a flight to New York is leaving on Friday afternoon, so I'm assuming from her info that Tracey is due to leave on that day."

"Man, I suggest you leave that girl alone. Pussy has a strange way of making a brother lose focus."

"Yeah, you right, but I think I have it under control."

"Don't be too sure, baby boy. I done seen brothers turn against one another over a female."

Ice laughed. "Ain't no pussy that good, bro."

Shortman shrugged. "Hey, I'm just hippin' you to the game. You can eat it or shit it out. Your choice, soul brother."

Airstead approached and took a seat. "How's my boy?" He kissed Ice on the cheek. Ice wiped his face in embarrassment.

"Damn, Pop, don't you think I'm a little too old for bedtime kisses?"

Airstead wrapped his arm around him and pulled him closer. "That's why I love you, son, because you remind me of myself when I was your age." He slapped his cheek softly, then got to his feet. "I have some business to handle in the back. Shorty, see me when you guys finish up." He turned and vanished into the crowd.

Kaila approached and put a drink on the table. "This is from the young lady in the red dress." She pointed across the room. He looked over and met eyes with a brown-skinned woman with a short haircut that fit her beautiful face perfectly. She blew a kiss.

Shortman laughed. "Boy, you got more whores than Iceberg Slim. You better wear a raincoat or you gonna die smoking." Ice laughed.

"Do you want me to send her over?" Kaila asked curiously.

"Does a bear shit in the woods and wipe his ass with a fluffy white rabbit? Hell yeah, I want you to send her over." He laughed. Kaila walked over to where she was seated and whispered something in her ear.

Shortman fixed his tie, then looked at Ice. "Hey, little brother, I think you gotta pass those lower half extremities to the original gangsta when you get done with her. Look at the curves on baby girl." He was admiring her as she approached. Ice got to his feet and took her hand and kissed it.

98

She smiled. "My name is Coco, and your name is Aldolphus aka the Iceman."

Ice and Shortman looked at one another and began to laugh. "I'm sorry. Do I know you?"

"Everyone knows who you are." At that very moment, a husky tall, dark male with a bald head approached and snatched Coco by the hair.

"What the fuck you doing, whore, trying to find a dick to suck?"

She grabbed his wrist and tried to break his strong grip. "Stop it, Bruno. You're hurting me."

"Shut up, cunt." He slapped her across the mouth, causing her lip to bleed.

Ice leaped to his feet. "Can't you see the woman's with me?"

Bruno reached into his jacket and pulled out a .40 caliber Desert Eagle and pointed it at Ice. "Don't roll up on me like you Neil Dellacroce or some motherfuckin' body. You better ask around, young boy, and check my rep for putting bitches in ditches." Shortman thought of pulling out and blasting but quickly changed his mind. Bruno continued with his diatribe, "Now I suggest you sit your pretty little ass down and stay out of grown folks' business."

Shortman placed his hand on Ice's shoulder. "Not yet, baby boy," he whispered. Ice took a seat. Bruno pulled Coco and vanished into the crowd.

"Don't worry. You will get your chance at redemption before the night is over. One thing that I've learned in this game is to always do your dirt with hands that hide from the sun."

"I know, but I can't just let that mark-ass nigga just chump me like that." Ice sounded sour.

"He didn't chump you. He thinks that he did and so does anyone else who was watching, and that's why we chill until the time is right. My old man was a southern gangster and taught to never pull your gun if you didn't plan to use it."

Ice smirked. "I think I'm feeling you, Shorty. Thanks for pulling my coat because that baldheaded bitch almost caught a dirt nap for testing my gangsta."

"Hey, it ain't no need to thank me, little brother. We in this thing together, right?" He extended his hand and they shook. Shortman was what you would call a game-tight brother from the ghetto, and he loved Ice like a brother. "Here, pick yourself up." Shortman slid the silver case across the table. Ice opened it and snorted two lines.

Irene approached, dressed in a tight-fitting blue dress. "Have you guys seen Airstead yet tonight?"

"Yep, he's in the back office, but I ain't letting your beautiful face out of my sight until you have a dance with me." Ice got to his feet and pulled Irene out onto the dance floor. They danced to three songs before he let her go. He went back to his seat with a hint of sweat on his brow.

"Damn, baby boy, you look like you just got done fuckin'." Shortman laughed.

"If I was fuckin', believe me, you would be the first to know, Shorty." They both laughed and then in a flash, Ice turned colder than his name. His smile became a tight grimace.

"What's up, little brother?" Ice gave a sardonic smile.

"I just saw our little friend Bruno the Baldheaded Monk head into the bathroom."

They both began making their way through the crowd. Ice began to feel that same flutter that he had when he pulled the trigger for the first time in his life.

"Stay cool, baby boy. Just go in and handle your business, and I'll cover the door." Shortman blocked the entrance. Ice walked into the bathroom and immediately pulled his weapon. He scanned the room quickly, and no one was in sight. He knelt and looked under the stalls and smiled as he saw the wine-colored gator shoes worn by Bruno. As he passed each stall, he could hear his own heartbeat become louder in his ear. Bruno sat on the toilet, unaware of what was about to take place. The door being kicked in caught him totally off guard, then he found himself looking into the blue eyes that had come to claim his life.

"You should've killed me when you had the chance."

Bruno went for his weapon, but it was too late. The two shots echoed in the bathroom and were only muffled by the club music.

Bruno sat slumped on the toilet with his brains painted on the wall behind. Ice put away his gun and calmly left the murder scene. Who would've thought that the sensitive eleven-year-old child that had witnessed the murder of his parents would become the same kind of monster that he feared: heartless, diabolical, and ruthless.

CHAPTER 4

IT WAS EARLY IN THE afternoon when Ice pulled into the parking lot of the airport. He had to see Tracey again, even if it was for the last time. Even if she was going to turn her back to him, they both shared a mutual love that wouldn't die overnight, and maybe, just maybe, she would reevaluate the situation upon seeing him in the flesh. His only fear was that he was too late. He walked through the glass doors and began making his way through the crowded airport, shoving some people when he deemed appropriate. He aggressively jumped the long line and took some heat from some of the people waiting.

"Did the flight to New York City leave yet?" he asked the woman behind the counter.

She looked at her monitor. "That flight is boarding right now at gate number 10."

He turned and ran as fast as he could. As he approached, he could see Tracey standing in a short line.

"Tracey! Yo, Tracey!" he yelled. She turned and saw Ice approaching. He took her by the hand. "How could you leave without saying goodbye to me?" Tears formed in her eyes as she removed her hand from his grip.

"I'm sorry, miss, but you need to be getting to your seat," said a stewardess walking up the ramp. Tracey looked at Ice, and for a moment, they were frozen in time.

"I'm saying goodbye right now, Aldolphus." She turned and began to walk.

"Do you mean forever?"

She stopped and faced him once more. "Yes, forever, Aldolphus, forever," she whispered.

The gate closed, and he stood, wearing sadness draped upon his face like a shroud. Tears grew behind his lids, but he blinked them away, allowing them to soak the flames of his burning heart. He walked over to the window. From the short distance, he met eyes with Tracey. Her face was flushed and tear streaked. They looked at one another for what seemed like an eternity, speaking terms of endearment with their eyes. There was so much more left to say and no time to do it. Tracey reached up and slowly closed the shade.

He stood for a moment, then turned on his heel, for he knew within his shattered heart that this chapter would remain an unfinished one until he and Tracey met again.

CHAPTER 5

AS THE YEARS PASSED, ICE had become everything that Airstead had groomed him to be: a thug, hustler, gangster, and blackhearted man. When he walked into a room, his presence spoke confidence and fearless acrimony. He had also developed a gambling problem over the years, and losing was something he never took lightly. He was only twenty-one, but his reputation was growing legendary wings.

It was 5:00 p.m. when Ice drove his late-model Jaguar up the driveway to the mansion. He looked at himself in the mirror and rubbed his full beard, which he had now begun to wear as a fashion statement. In the distance, he could see an ambulance with flashing lights. He saw Irene crying uncontrollably, with Shortman trying to console her. He leaped from the vehicle.

"What in the hell happened?" He grabbed one of the EMTs by the collar.

"Calm down, sir. Mr. Airstead just had a mild fainting spell, and we are just taking him in to run some tests."

Ice pushed the man backward aggressively into the truck. "Let me tell you: if anything happens to one gorgeous hair on my father's head, then it's buckwheats for you. Is that understood?"

Shortman grabbed his arm. "Come on. Let's go. It ain't worth it, baby boy." He pulled him away from the EMT.

Irene stood at the back of the ambulance, looking in at an unconscious Airstead wearing an oxygen mask. Ice put his arm around her. "It's going to be all right. Daddy is a soldier. Whatever is going on, he'll pull through."

An hour had passed since they had arrived at the hospital. Irene sat resting her head on Shortman's shoulder, while Ice paced back and forth like a nervous wreck. The air was empty and still, and Ice felt his heart crashing like thunder in his chest. A tall blond woman with glasses entered the room.

"Hello, I'm Dr. Bower."

Irene got to her feet in a hurry. "How is my husband?"

The question seemed frozen in time before the doctor took a deep breath. "I'm afraid your husband is suffering from terminal brain cancer, and he doesn't have very long to live."

Irene collapsed to the floor. Ice rushed over and lifted her up into his arms.

"It can't be true. It just can't be!" she cried. Ice kissed her tears gently.

"Don't talk. Just let me hold you."

He helped her over to a chair and rested her head on his shoulder. Shortman continued to talk with Dr. Bower and get more details on Airstead's condition. Minutes later, Ice found himself outside room 302, where Airstead was being kept. Bower had told them that he had requested to see Irene and Shortman first and then Aldolphus.

He sat patiently outside the room and closed his eyes, allowing the memories to rain down on him. He was twelve years old again and seated in the car next to Airstead.

*　　*　　*　　*　　*

The rain began to fall slowly at first then at a rapid pace. Airstead stopped at the light.

"Are you always this quiet?" he asked, smiling at Aldolphus.

"I'm just scared after seeing you shoot that guy back there."

"You have no reason to be afraid of me. I shot that kid over you. I know all about what happened to your parents, and hopefully you never have to worry about that sort of thing ever happening again."

*　　*　　*　　*　　*

The door to the hospital room opened, bringing Ice back to age twenty-one. He got to his feet as Irene and Shortman stepped out into the hall. Irene gave a tired smirk as she passed. As Ice stepped into the dimly lit room, he could hear the constant beeping of a monitor, and the silhouette from behind the curtain created a strange atmosphere. He opened it and stepped in next to the bed. Seeing his caretaker and role model lying there helpless was like a knife to his heart. Ice had always known him to be a strong and determined man, and now he appeared weak and vulnerable—his blue eyes had become a dull glow. He forced a smile.

"How's my baby boy doing?" His voice was slow and husky.

Ice took his hand into his. "How are you, Pop?"

Airstead chuckled weakly. "How am I? I'm dying, so I guess I'm doing pretty well."

Ice instantly felt the water building behind his lids. "You're not going to die, Pop. Stop talking like that."

Airstead coughed. "Just do me a favor, son."

"I will do anything for you, Pop. You know that." Airstead closed his eyes briefly, then slowly opened them.

"Make me some grandkids, and if you have a baby boy, name him after me. Can you promise me that?"

Ice squeezed his hand. "I promise, Pop."

CHAPTER 6

Cut with a Spade

AFTER LEAVING THE HOSPITAL, ICE dropped Irene at Kaila's, then he and Shortman headed across town to Fast Eddie's house. Eddie was an ex-con turned gambler, and every Friday he hosted a popular card game called Chicago Diamonds. He lived in a nice five-bedroom flat in Jasper Circle.

The moon was just appearing from behind the black heavens. They pulled up to Eddie's.

"Do you got your bankroll?" he asked, looking at Shortman.

"You know it, baby boy."

"Well, let's go take these chumps' money."

They both got out of the car, walked up the steps, then tapped on the door. An attractive Spanish woman answered.

"Hey, Carol, what's going down?" They stepped into the house, and both men greeted her with a kiss on the cheek.

"Nothing much. Eddie is in the cardroom, and I'm on my way out. I will catch you guys later." She headed out of the door. They walked down the hall, then entered a smoke-filled reefer room. The jukebox in the corner played an old Marvin Gaye song.

Eddie was a brown-skinned brother with a processed hairdo. He looked up and smiled.

"Just the two people I wanted to see: Mutt and Jeff." He laughed as he dealt cards to the two other men seated at the table.

"Hey, Red, what's the score?" He looked at his partner. Red was a fair-skinned brother with freckles and red hair who had done time with Eddie in the slammer.

"It's five up, meaning winner takes all." He laughed. The other two occupants were also known players: Poky Pig and Ajax were their names. Ice and Shortman took a seat on the couch and looked on.

"Hey, Poky, you and Ajax need to hurry up and take that ass whipping because me and Ice are starting to get impatient," said Shortman, laughing.

"Stay your short ass on the sideline while real players is on the field," Poky responded.

Ice reached into his pocket, pulled out a bag of powder, took a snort, then handed it to Shortman. "It's going to be a long night, so you might as well pick yourself up."

"I can dig it, soul brother, but not if we break these fools like we plan on."

Eddie jumped to his feet with energy. "This game is over." He slammed his final card on the table.

Ajax shook his head in disgust and slowly got to his feet. "It's time to pay the banker," said Red, opening a paper bag. Poky Pig and Ajax dropped their bankrolls into it.

"Now y'all know the way out." Eddie laughed, pointing toward the door.

"This ain't over yet, Eddie. We'll be back on Friday for a rematch," said Ajax, walking to the door, followed closely by Poky.

"That's fine with me, Soul brother. Just bring your fine-ass girlfriend with you in case I break y'all again. I love collateral especially when a pussy is attached." He laughed.

"Fuck you, Eddie." Then he closed the door behind.

Shortman gave Ice a nudge. "Our turn." And they made their way over to the table and sat down. Fast Eddie began to shuffle the cards, and it was evident why he had been given the nickname. His hands were a blur.

"We getting ready to send y'all boys home broke." He chuckled while dealing the cards. The first hand went to Red and Eddie and so did the second and third, but before the fourth, Ice caught the smooth movement of Eddie flipping a card under his sleeve. Fire shot through his veins. He jumped to his feet, flipped the table, then pulled his weapon.

"You slimy fuckin' chicken hawk!" he snapped.

Red reached for his gun, but Shortman already had one pointing in his direction. "Don't try it, Red Fox, or I'm going to turn off your electric." He smiled.

"Look, Ice, it ain't whatcha think, baby boy."

Ice walked over to Eddie. "Why would you play the ace of hearts, when you know that I cut with a spade?"

He ruthlessly shoved the barrel of his gun into Eddie's mouth, knocking out several of his teeth. Eddie screamed in agony, and blood trickled down the nose of the smoke pole.

"Look at me, Eddie. Remember this face when you wake up from the dead." He pulled the trigger. The blast exploded the back of Eddie's neck, and his body fell from the chair and hit the floor. Ice stood over the body. "Now the next time you think about cheating, make sure that you choose the right one." He kicked his lifeless body viciously, then turned and glared at Red. "Do you see what kind of friends you have? Like the Bible says: 'Bad association spoils useful habits.'" He laughed, then nodded at his friend.

Shortman took aim. "Say a silent prayer, motherfucker." The hot slug took out Red's eye socket, killing him instantly.

They filled the bag with all the money, then left the residence. To gain money and power were the second and third laws of the blood game, but to be able to pull the trigger without feelings was by far the number one commandment.

CHAPTER 7

ICE PULLED INTO THE PARKING garage of the casino. It had been seven days since Airstead had been given a death sentence, and Ice was still trying to come to terms with the fact that the man who raised him was going to die, and that his eyes would someday soon be bloodshot from tears as he would find himself in the cemetery talking to the dirt. He had now taken over running the casino and found it overwhelming without the backbone of his idol.

He took a pickup of powder, checked his eyes in the mirror, got out of the car, and quickly headed for the back entrance of the club. He was in no mood to face a crowd. He pulled a set of keys from his pocket, then entered Airstead's office. He turned on the lights and glanced over at the poster of Airstead, Shortman, Irene, and himself on the opening night of the casino and club. He forced a smirk and flopped down in the chair behind the desk.

Life's no good, he thought to himself, taking a deep breath and running his fingers through his hair. He snorted more powder, then suddenly had the vision of Airstead lying in that bed and barely living, then of Sofia and Clevio. The segments continued to flash like a nonstop strobe light. He gripped his head between his palms and tried to abolish his thoughts with brainpower, but they seemed to become more intense. His heart fought against his chest and sweat formed on his brow.

Then a voice that he had never heard began to whisper, *Go ahead and blow your fucking brains out. Just kill the memories, and your pain will go away.* He pulled his gun from the holster under his jacket and placed it into his mouth and cocked back the hammer.

Suddenly the phone began to ring.

Don't answer it. Kill the memories, said the voice again.

He felt the tremble of his own hand, then he slammed the weapon onto the desk and picked up the phone. "Hello." His voice was empty.

"Yo, what's up, baby boy?" came the voice from the other end.

"Nothing much, Shorty. Where are you exactly?"

Shortman laughed. "I'm down on the lower level of the club in the pool getting my freak on with two hourglass-shaped beauties. You should join us unless you need me for something."

"Naw, Shorty, I'm cool, but while I'm thinking about it, I was wondering if you could close up the nightclub for me tonight and get Monster and Noodles to help you out. I ain't feeling so good and thinking about mashing out early tonight."

"Don't sweat it, Ice. I got it covered. You should probably go and see how Irene is holding up anyway."

"Thanks, Shorty. I appreciate you." And then the line went dead.

Ice pulled out his keys and searched until he found the one that opened Airstead's desk. Shortman had just saved his life; if it hadn't been from that phone call, there was no doubt that his brains would've been splattered against the back of his bulletproof chair. Those thoughts now somehow seemed foolish and cynical.

He opened the drawer and was in the process of searching for Airstead's ledger book when he came across a black-and-white photo of Airstead holding two twin babies. On the back of the photo, in faded words, it read "My boys." He jumped to his feet, dropped the photo into his pocket, then exited out of the back.

Once in the car, he snorted another mountain of powder. As he pulled into the street, his vision became blurred, making the cars in front of him merge momentarily. He ran a red light and was almost sideswiped by a pickup truck. Thousands of shattered thoughts ran through his mind in short and confusing segments; everything seemed so far from being reality. He made a sharp turn, then ran two more red lights, and then pulled into the hospital lot. He put the car into park, then leaped from the vehicle. He pushed through the glass doors, then headed down the hall.

A nurse that was seated at a desk got to her feet as he passed. "Sir? May I help you? Sir!" she yelled.

Ice was deaf to everything around him. He pushed the button for the elevator and waited only seconds before turning on his heel and walking through the stairwell doors. He climbed the steps four at a time; beads of sweat could be seen on his brow by the time he reached the third floor.

As he made his way into Airstead's room, his heart pounded, and his hands had a slight tremble. The beeping of the monitor seemed louder against the quiet of the night. He pulled back the curtain and stepped behind it. Airstead looked old and bewildered: his head was almost full of gray hair, and his skin looked dry and pale.

Ice grabbed his hand, "Pop, I'm here," he whispered.

Airstead's eyes opened, then shut, then opened again. "I didn't think I would get a visitor this late." His voice sounded weaker than before.

Ice dropped a tear. "Pop, I need to know something."

Airstead struggled to get some air into his lungs. "Tell me your wish, son."

Ice had already prepared himself for a sermon of lies, but a lie had to be better than not knowing any of the truth. He reached and pulled out the photo and placed it into Airstead's hand. He glared at it for what seemed like an eternity, then suddenly he broke into a quiet sobbing.

"I'm sorry, Aldolphus, I'm so sorry," he cried.

Ice had never seen him so weak, and the sight of it was like having a knife twisted into his heart. Airstead gripped his hand tightly.

"Listen closely to what I'm about to say. It started when I was just out of high school when Sofia told me that she was pregnant."

*   *   *   *   *

Flashback

Airstead pulled in front of Trinidad's Ballroom on Compton Avenue. Trinidad was a Mexican drug dealer who ran most of the drugs in the city. A young Airstead looked over at his best friend, Clevio. They had been friends since elementary, and now both had landed jobs as runners for Trinidad. Business was going well for the two young men who were freshly out of high school.

"You ready to move up the ranks another notch?" He studied his friend closely.

Clevio smiled. "I was born ready, my boy," he responded, getting out of the car.

They entered the building and were met by a husky tall Italian man. Without words, they both turned and placed their hands on the tops of their heads. He frisked them roughly.

"All right. Mr. Trinidad is in the back." He gestured with his thumb.

They walked back to a booth where two men sat. One was short and stocky with curly hair. He had a chubby face and deep piercing eyes. The other was a tall Mexican with a long ponytail. He got to his feet and embraced both boys.

"How's my favorite rebels?" he asked in his heavy accent.

Airstead smiled. "Everything is cool, Trinidad. Just trying to make the best out of a bad situation." They sat down.

"Hey, Sonny, get two drinks for my boys here." He gestured toward the other man at the table. He got to his feet and glared at the young upstarts. Sonny was Trinidad's best soldier, but he harbored envy in his heart at how his boss treated the two youngsters. Trinidad lit a cigar.

"So how is Sofia?" Directing his question at Airstead.

"She's fine. Just waiting to have my twin boys."

"Well, make sure you keep my name in mind when she has them." Trinidad laughed.

Sonny returned and slammed the drinks onto the table aggressively, causing one of them to spill a little. "Damn, Sonny, if we had known that you were on your period, we would've brought you some tampons," said Clevio, laughing.

Sonny pulled a snub-nosed revolver from his holster and put it to the young upstart's head. "You better watch your fuckin' ass around me, boy, because I don't like the way you smell anyway, Clev."

Trinidad reached up and took the weapon from his hand and calmly tucked it into his waistline. Then he quickly pulled Sonny by his tie, bringing him to a seat. He slapped him viciously across the face several times.

"Don't you ever in your fucking life pull a weapon on one my workers! Now get the hell out of my sight." He shoved him backward. Clevio watched him walk away and gave a slight smirk.

"Now let's get down to business."

Trinidad sat a black case on the table. "There's two kilos of china white in here, and it needs to be delivered to the old banana factory at 7:00 a.m. tomorrow. You're going to be meeting with a tall blond Russian girl named Sasha. She is one dangerous bitch, so wear your vest just in case things get heated." He next turned his attention to Clev. "And, Clevio, you know your job: stay in the car with the Uzi, and if something even smells wrong, you take out everything moving. Understood?"

Clevio smiled. "I got it, boss. Trust me on that."

"How about you, Airstead? Do you have any problems with the plan?"

He took a sip of his drink before responding. "It sounds game tight to me, boss. I have no problems."

"Good. You boys are going to move up fast in this game." Trinidad got to his feet. "Give my regards to Sofia." He extended his hand and they shook.

The night was chilly and wet from the flow of rain as Airstead pulled his 1969 Chevy onto the street.

"It looks like the night is over." Clevio reclined his seat.

Airstead chuckled. "Your life was almost over when Sonny pulled out that pistol on you."

"Man, fuck Sonny. I ain't thinking about him. He's a raw bitch. You saw the way Trinidad slapped him around."

"Yeah, the word in your sentence. Trinidad slapped him, not you." Airstead laughed. Then he glanced at his watch. "Oh shit. We're late."

He pulled into the southside projects where they both lived.

"Late for what?"

"Sofia's little party for my babies, you idiot." They jumped from the car and headed up the sidewalk.

They could hear the loud music and laughter coming from the other side of the door. Airstead fumbled his keys and Clevio laughed.

"Don't get scared now. Your ass should've been home hours ago." His laughter continued.

"Hold this." Airstead handed Clevio the case containing the drugs. He opened the door and stepped into the crowded room.

"You're late, mister," said Sofia, standing akimbo.

"I know, baby."

He kissed her lips. "How's my babies doing?" He rubbed her large stomach.

"They are kicking my ass royally."

He put his arm around her. "You've got two months, baby, and then it's all over."

As they walked through the party, some of the other people gave high fives to the two notorious upstarts.

"Do you want something to eat?" Sofia asked, looking at Airstead.

"Yeah, how about you on a platter with peach cobbler for dessert." He winked.

Sofia shoved him in the chest. "You better behave. You wore this pussy out enough, and now look at the result: double trouble." She rubbed her stomach, then continued into the kitchen.

Clevio wrapped his arm around Airstead's shoulder and leaned toward his ear. "That's a fine lady you have there, Airstead. I hope you marry her."

"Yeah, and I hope you marry her sister, Irene." He laughed.

"You speak of the devil, and here she comes."

Irene approached. "Are y'all talking about me?" She placed one hand on the hip of her shapely figure.

"Naw, Irene, I'm just trying to figure out why Clevio is scared to rap to you."

Irene laughed. "Well, ain't it obvious that your boy ain't never had a real woman before?"

Airstead laughed harder. "Oh shit, Clev, you gonna let her rank you like that?"

Clevio shifted his weight. "Girl, I'd fuck you so good that I would make your soul shake hands with your spirit." Everyone erupted with laughter.

"Well, you know what they say about them fools that's always talking about what they can do in bed. Nine times out of ten, they got a little dick complex." She held her thumb and forefinger inches apart. Airstead laughed at Irene's rebuttal.

Clevio shifted his weight again. "Man, I then heard enough from Short and Spunky. I'm mixing with the crowd." He handed Airstead the case, then turned on his heel.

"He is such a coward," she said, shaking her head.

"Do you want a beer, Airstead?"

"I do, and tell your pregnant sister that I said, 'Hurry up with that food.'" He headed over to the card table where a game of dominoes was being played. "Any room for a real playa?" He directed his question at a dark-complexioned girl with glasses.

"Damn, ain't you rude? You don't even speak no more," her response was sarcastic.

Airstead squinted as if he were struggling with the young woman's identity. "Damn, Janice, I'm sorry. I couldn't recognize you behind those Coke-bottle glasses." He laughed.

She tilted her head, then looked over the rim of her glasses. "You are not funny. Not in the smallest way."

"I'm just fuckin' with you, Janice. You know that you're my peeps." He kissed her cheek.

Minutes later.

"Clevio, get away from me. You had too much to drink!" snapped Sofia, pushing him backward into the stove.

"You wasn't saying that a few months ago when I fucked you."

"Clevio, stop it! What happened between us was a onetime deal and could never happen again, and besides that, if Airstead was to ever find out, he would probably kill us both."

"So what are you saying? The dick was weak? Huh, Sofia, is that what you're saying?"

She clenched her teeth. "No. What I'm saying is that we are playing this a little too close for comfort. Maybe after I have my babies, things will be different."

"Different for who?" yelled a voice. Clevio and Sofia looked over into the face of a raging Airstead; guilt and exposure draped their expressions like a wet rag.

"Honey, let me explain." Before her next word could exit her mouth, he slapped her viciously, knocking her to the floor.

"I trusted you, Clev, just like a brother." He gripped him by the collar, then whirled him across the room.

Sofia slowly got her feet, then entered into a frenzy of hysteria. "Help me! Oh god, help me!" She ran into the other room.

Clevio swung a hook, but Airstead ducked, then quickly delivered a machine gun of blows to his midsection, then brought up his knee into his forehead. The dizziness clouded his thoughts. Airstead gripped his shirt and the back of his pants and in one motion lifted him and tossed him headfirst through the large glass window. Onlookers filled the room. Airstead walked into the backyard just as Clevio was struggling to get to his feet.

"I should've pushed up your due date a long time ago."

He kicked him in the face, knocking him back to the ground. Then he pulled his smoke pole and aimed it at his friend.

"Please, Airstead, don't throw your life away like this," cried Irene.

Her pleas were followed by several more from the onlookers, and then suddenly sirens could be heard approaching in the distance. He turned quickly and took aim at the crowd of people.

"Back the fuck up! I said back the fuck up!"

The crowd parted like the Red Sea, and Airstead raced through like Moses. He made his way into the house, snatched up the case containing the drugs, then jumped behind the wheel and peeled off.

That day was the start of a war that some would die fighting and others would live, battling the demons of yesterday that had come to haunt their dreams.

CHAPTER 8

AIRSTEAD PULLED IN THE SMALL lot of Jake's Motel. It was a shabby, low-budget place that was mostly used by pimps and prostitutes. He sat momentarily behind the wheel and reflected on the night's events.

I should've blown his head off, he said to himself. Then he thought about returning and finishing the job. He grabbed the case off the seat, then entered the motel lobby.

The inside looked like a converted house. An elderly black man with gray hair and a chubby face stood behind an old kitchen counter.

"I would like a single room, please," Airstead said gently.

The old man laughed. "You just made it, youngster. You get the finest room I have. It's the presidential suite." He dangled the keys in his face, and Airstead reached for them. "Not so fast, youngster." He snatched the keys backward. "That's twenty dollars a night with a five-dollar key deposit." He held out his palm. Airstead sighed then reached into his pocket. The man looked nosy as he shuffled through his large bankroll. After paying for two nights, he headed up the stairs and down the hall and opened the door to room 4. As he stepped inside, the smell was dry with old mothballs. He turned on the light, then chuckled.

"If this is the best room, then I would hate to see the worst." The walls were cracked, and several roaches could be seen crawling on the wooden floor. He shut and locked the door, then took a seat on the bed. "How could you do this to me, Sofia? How could you?" He ran his fingers through his hair.

Sofia sat on the couch with her head in her hands and tears running down her face.

"How could I tear my family apart like this, Irene?"

She looked up at her younger sister. She took a seat and wrapped her arm around her sibling and caressed her. "It's going to be okay, sis. Airstead still loves you. I know he does," she whispered.

Clevio entered the room and took a seat on her other side. "I'm sorry, Sofia. I had a little too much to drink."

Her head snapped in his direction. "Get out, you rotten bastard! Isn't it enough that you ruined my life? Get out, you son of a bitch!" she yelled.

Clevio got to his feet and headed out of the house; anger and frustration shooting through his mind like a strong bolt of lightning. *I want revenge,* he said to himself. *I gotta get rid of Airstead for good. That's the only way that I'll have Sofia.* He smiled at his own vindictive thoughts. He crossed the street, then picked up the receiver on the pay phone and took a deep breath. *I have to do this, Airstead. It's the only way to make it right.* He dialed a number, and it rang twice before a female voice answered.

"Police department."

"Yes, I have some information about a drug deal going down in the morning."

Airstead picked up the phone and dialed the number to Trinidad's Ballroom. After several rings, a voice answered, "Hello, this is Trinidad's. How may we help you?"

"Yeah, this is Airstead, and I need to speak to Trinidad about some important business." There was a pause, then a sigh was let out.

"I'll transfer you." The phone rang, then was answered quickly. "Hello?"

"Yeah, Trinidad, this is Airstead. I ran into some problems."

"What kind of problems, Papi?"

"Well, Clev ain't going to be able to make the job tomorrow, so I was wondering if you could send in another man." There was a long pause as if Trinidad was deep in thought.

"Here is what I'll do, Papi. Do you have your vest?"

"Yeah, I'm wearing it now." He knocked on the body armor under his shirt.

"Okay, I will send another player, but you won't know that he is there. He will have you covered from all angles." Then he hung up.

Airstead chuckled for he knew that he would be alone on the job; something in Trinidad's voice told him that the man felt uneasy about something in their telephone conversation and thought that Airstead was conjuring up a plan of his own. He relaxed back onto the bed and gazed at the ceiling. Tonight was like a nightmare.

Death is conceivable, but the betrayal of a loved one is like having your body pumped full of lead thorns.

CHAPTER 9

AIRSTEAD WOKE UP THE NEXT morning and checked his watch. He had an hour before he was due to meet Sasha at the old factory to make the drop for Trinidad. He took a cold shower, then dressed carefully, putting on his bulletproof vest and then his jeans, shirt, and dinner coat. He tucked his smoke pole into his waist, then checked himself in the mirror. The morning sky was cloudy as he made his way to the motel parking lot. The butterflies began to flutter almost instantly in his stomach and sweat formed on his palms. He started the vehicle and made a U-turn out into the street. Memories of Sofia walked the steps of his mind, and he wondered where it all went wrong.

He stopped at a red light and drummed his fingers on the wheel. The light turned green just as the sun peeked out from behind the clouds. He headed down Jackson Avenue, then made a left onto Lincoln Drive. He passed two stores, then made a right turn onto Brentwood Street. He slowly passed the factory, then pulled into the rear parking area of the building and drove up the ramp leading into the building. It was relatively empty and had a gloomy look. He scanned the large area for signs of life; there were none. He reached and grabbed the case off the seat, then climbed from the car.

The breeze entered and chilled his body. Suddenly, the doors at the far end of the building began to open, and a red BMW entered. It had limousine tint, making impossible to see inside. It stopped about ten feet away from him, then the engine shut off. Time seemed to freeze like a movie on pause, then suddenly the passenger door opened and out stepped a red high-heeled foot. He studied the ankle and noticed it was shining with diamonds. Then the body appeared from behind the door. Airstead was astonished at the tall woman's beauty; her hair was cut in a short style, and it was blond in color. She wore sunglasses and a tight-fitting leather dress that rested just above her knees, showing off her perfectly shaped legs. Her breasts were firm and protruded gracefully above the tight leather.

She walked slowly and almost catlike in his direction, and in her hand was a silver case that probably was housing the buy money. He remembered wondering how this extremely attractive Russian woman could be dangerous in any way besides the bedroom. The thought brought a smirk to his face. She looked him from head to toe.

"Do you have the ice cream?" she asked in a strong accent.

"I have it right here." He held it in front. "Do you have the money?"

Sasha smiled while licking her lips seductively. "I've got the money right here." She rubbed her case on his crotch.

Then came a loud crashing sound. "Freeze! FBI. Drop the shit and put your hands in the air!" Men dressed in riot gear and suits seemed to swarm from almost every direction.

"You American bastard, you set me up!" Sasha reached under her skirt and pulled out a Beretta 9 mm. Airstead was caught totally off guard as she fired two shots at his chest. He fell to floor.

The BMW came to life and attempted to run down a crowd of agents, but the firepower quickly turned the coupe into a convertible, and it crashed into the wall and burst into flames. Sasha began firing more shots. Two of her bullets struck and killed two agents, but her attempts at warfare were in vain. The bullets began to fill her body; each one dimming the light of life as they found a resting place. Her body completed two 360-degree turns before it collapsed to the floor, lifeless and aware of nothing, with smoke escaping from each hole.

CHAPTER 10

BUTTERFLIES AND THE EARLY SYMPTOMS of diarrhea filled his stomach as Airstead made his way into the county jail. He was barely out of high school and was booked on a possession charge. He couldn't help but hear the catcalls and obscenities that were being hurled his way while being escorted down the prison hall by two guards.

"Open cell 228," the guard said into his communication device. The door opened slowly. He stepped into the small six-by-nine-foot cell, carrying only his bed linens.

He took a seat, then rested his head in his palms. Depression and the fear of the unknown masked any positive thoughts that he tried to muster.

"Hey, homie, it ain't that bad." Airstead looked up into the face of his cellmate, who was stretched out on the top bunk, looking over the edge.

"It's bad enough," he responded.

The boy swung his feet off the side of the bed, then leaped to the floor. He was extremely short, brown-skinned, and sported a Caesar haircut. He took a seat on the stool across from Airstead.

"My name is Granville Rollins, but my friends call me Shortman." He extended his hand.

"I'm Airstead Gaddafi." They shook.

"Gaddafi, huh, are you political?" Shortman's question was serious.

"Not political at all. I guess my family were fans of the Libyan uprising." He chuckled. "And what about you? What kind of coun-try-ass name is Granville Rollins?"

Shortman chuckled. "My family is originally from the South, so that's where it comes from. So whatcha in for, Airstead?"

He took a deep breath. "I got busted with two kilos of White Girl."

Shortman's eyes grew three sizes. "Damn, celly, I hate to be the one to tell you, but you're about to get some serious numbers."

Airstead laughed. "Trust me, it ain't the time that I'm worried about. It's my pregnant girlfriend that has me twisted."

"What's up with her? Don't tell me you pussy whipped."

Airstead shook his head. "It's a long story. So what's your story? What brings you to this beautiful resort?"

Shortman smiled. "I'm in for gang-related homicide, but I should beat it in front of twelve. You know, no witness, no crime." Airstead nodded.

"Chow time! Chow time!" said the voice over the loudspeaker. The cell doors began to open.

"Come on, let's go eat." Shorty got to his feet with Airstead following close behind.

The prison lunchroom was loud, and all the blue uniforms mingling in one place looked like a mechanic's convention.

"This is the place we call home," said Shortman, looking back at his cellmate. He chuckled then grabbed a metal tray and headed through the line. They were serving potatoes and some weird-looking kind of meat.

"What the hell is this?" Airstead picked it up with his plastic fork.

Shortman turned and smiled. "It's rat meat probably. Why? You don't want it?" He held his tray toward Airstead.

"Damn, Shorty, I was just asking. I didn't say that I was going on a diet." They both laughed and headed over and took a seat at a table.

"So do you got a paid lawyer or a public defender?"

Airstead found the question funny and very well put together. "I ain't got nothing yet. I'm gonna try and contact some of my peoples on the street and see what they come up with."

"I know some good attorneys. I have the list back in the cell if you want to check 'em out."

A husky Latin man approached and folded his arms across his chest. "You sittin' in my seat, white boy."

Airstead looked up into the man's face, then looked around the base of the chair stupidly. "I'm sorry, man. I don't see your name on this chair. In fact, I think you're in the wrong mess hall."

The other prisoners at the table chuckled and whispered among themselves. He reached and snatched Airstead up in the collar. "I'm going to knock every last one of your teeth off the hinges."

He drew back his fist, but before he could launch his assault, Airstead brought a knee up into his groin that bent him over like six fifteen. Then he quickly grabbed the tray of food off the table and took a major league swing at his face. Blood shot from his mouth and landed on a random shirt. Airstead took another swing, and this one put him to the ground. One of his friends jumped onto Airstead's back and attempted to put him into a chokehold, but Shortman reacted quickly and began raining shots to the other man's kidneys. The other prisoners shouted as the battle royal continued.

Guards ran over with nightsticks and began beating the four men until they had them separated and in cuffs. They ushered Airstead and Shortman down one hall while several other guards took the other men in the opposite direction. Several guards in black helmets surrounded them.

"So you motherfuckers want to start a riot, do you?"

Airstead studied closely, trying to determine who was speaking, but the dark helmets made it impossible. One of them stepped forward and shoved his nightstick into Shortman's midsection, instantly slumping him to the floor. The last thing that Airstead remembered seeing was the large stick that had struck his head and knocked him into a state of temporary sleep.

CHAPTER 11

AIRSTEAD WOKE UP TO DARKNESS and momentarily thought that he had somehow lost his vision. The small cell he was confined to was cold and wet.

This must be the hole, he thought to himself. He tried getting to his feet but a sharp pain in his back from the beating brought him to his knees. Suddenly the slot on his cell door opened and some light escaped, finally allowing him a little vision.

"Gaddafi, you got mail," said a voice.

He crawled over toward the light. A hand reached inside and handed him an envelope.

"I will leave your slot open for ten minutes so you can read your letter, and then I have to shut it down."

He held the letter closer to the light and saw that that it was from Irene Jackson. He opened it nervously, then began to read.

> Dear Airstead,
>
> I know I'm probably the last person that you expected to hear from, but when I heard about what happened, I knew that you would need support from at least one person. I'm sorry about what has happened between you and Sofia. Although she is my sister and I love her to death, I constantly tell her how wrong she is for what she has done to you. I hope that we can remain friends throughout this hideous ordeal, and I'm also hoping that you and Sofia can at least have a friendship for the kids' sakes. If it's okay with

you, I'd like to come and visit, and if there is anything that I can do, just let me know. I'm in your
corner, Airstead, and I'm here if you need me.

Love Always,
Lil Sis Irene

The kind words spoken in her letter turned his heart into a thousand smiles.

When he was finally released from the hole, he and Shorty were separated and each confined to a single-man cell. Airstead began spending his days in the gym playing ball or working out. The only time that he and Shorty could connect was during yard, which they had once a day. During that two hours of recreation, the two men built a friendship that could only be broken in death.

The day Irene came to visit, he dressed in new prison blues and combed his hair into a style. He entered the area and took a seat at one of the booths that had a telephone and twelve inches of thick glass. Minutes later, Irene walked in. She was dressed in a pair of firm-fitting jeans and a red blouse, and her hair was in a ponytail. She smiled as she picked up the phone.

"Long time, no see, stranger." Her tone sounded cute and pleasing to his ears.

"It ain't been that long. About sixty days and counting."

"I guess that's not too bad." She laughed.

Airstead took a deep breath. "Irene, you just don't know how much it means to me having you in my corner. I mean with all this nonsense going on and the stress attached to it, having someone like you in my life is a blessing."

"Don't worry, Airstead. I'm here for the duration. I told you that whatever you wish and need for, I'll be your genie in the bottle." She laughed.

"So how is Sofia?"

There was a pause as she studied closely. "Well, you know that she is due any day now, right?"

He nodded. "Yeah, I was trying not to remember. So did she decide on names yet for the boys?"

Irene smiled. "Yes, and I helped her."

"Well, what did you come up with?" He sounded anxious.

"Aldolphus and Amias," she blurted.

He sat quiet for a moment as the names sank in, then he smiled. "I like it, they have a Gaddafi ring to them."

"Oh, stop being conceited. I wonder if your head can fit through that door behind you." They both laughed.

"Naw, Irene, it ain't like that. I just learned to joke a lot just to keep from crying in this slaughterhouse."

"Is it really that bad in there?"

"Bad enough to hide your butt cheeks from a greasy man named Bubba Joe." They shared a laugh. "Seriously though, I'm a soldier and won't quit until this war is over."

"Do you have an attorney yet?" She changed the subject.

He sighed. "Not yet, but I was wondering if you could do me favor."

She moved closer to the window, giving him all her attention. "I'm all ears."

"Well, there is this Mexican that I was working for named Trinidad. He owns the ballroom near center city. I need for you to go and see him and let him know that I need his help or else the system is going to railroad me, and I'm damn sure not prepared to lay it down for the next twenty or something more outlandish."

"Don't worry. I will take care of it. You just stay strong and out of trouble until I get it handled."

The light began to flicker on and off, indicating the end of the visiting period.

"That was the quickest half of an hour that I've ever seen." She checked her watch, and Airstead got to his feet.

"Will I see you next visiting day?"

"Do you need to ask? You know that God willing, I will be here, and if everything goes well with Trinidad, then I'll be back earlier."

He smiled. "Thanks again, Irene. I won't forget it."

After the visit, he headed down the hall toward his cellblock with good thoughts. For a man in prison, knowing that he had some-one like Irene on his team fighting on his behalf was enough to give him the strength to run the extra mile. He thought of Sofia and wondered why she could never ingest his love completely, and how his best friend could betray him so easily.

CHAPTER 12

AIRSTEAD WALKED INTO THE YARD, looking forward to seeing Shortman. He leaned against the wall near the weight pile. Within a matter of minutes, his friend appeared.

"What's up, baby boy?" He stood next to Airstead.

"Nothing much, Shorty. How did things go at court?"

Shortman smiled. "It's looking good so far. Like I said before. No witnesses, no motherfuckin' crime. I still have a robbery beef to fight the max on that is two to five years according to my lawyer, so either way, I should come up."

Airstead nodded. "That's what it's all about, coming up. I'm trying to get the least time possible so I can get out there and make moves."

"What kinda moves are you talking about?"

Airstead studied his friend closely. "I ain't really sure yet, but I can tell you this much: I'm going to be a self-made millionaire before I'm thirty."

Shortman laughed. "Those are some pretty lofty goals, my boy."

"Well, if I don't believe in me, then who will?"

"I can feel you on that, baby boy. So I heard that you got a visit from a drop-dead gorgeous sista a few days ago?"

Airstead was astonished. "How did you hear about that?"

Shortman gave a devious smile before responding. "That's classified information, partner."

Airstead chuckled. "I can respect that from another gangster."

"I'm just fuckin' with you, man, but does she have a sister by any chance?"

"She has a sister for sure, but she's pregnant with my two sons that are due any day now."

Shortman gave a curious look. "Hold up. Let me get this straight. You're fuckin' both of them?"

"No, not at all. My girl crossed me for some chili chump—ass buster, and her little sister just been representin' and holding down on the business side of things." They talked for a little while longer and vowed that they would stay in touch.

Airstead entered his cell and picked up the letter that had been placed under his door. He smiled as he realized it was from Irene. He took a seat at the small metal desk, opened it, and began to read.

Dear Airstead,

> A lot has happened over the past few days, so relax and read carefully. Sofia went into labor a few days back, and you are now the father of two baby boys. The names are the ones I shared with you earlier. Clevio has been hanging around a lot, pretending to be so in love with Sofia. She is so stupid sometimes that it drives me crazy. I'm also trying to convince her to visit you with the kids after a few weeks, but you know how stubborn she is.

> The boys are gorgeous and look a lot like you, especially the eye color and the little bit of curly hair on their heads. I will get you a photo before your first contact visit, and maybe then you can take some pictures with them.

> Now for the bad news. After our visit, I went to see that guy Trinidad. At first, he wouldn't see me, and then I told his bouncer that it was about you. Let me tell you that he's one ignorant and arrogant son of a bitch. For the first twenty minutes, he talked about himself and about how sexy I looked, then when I changed the subject back to you, he went off about how you knew the job was hard when you took it, and that he had got-

ten wind that you were trying to cut a deal with the feds. I called him a liar, and then he flew into a rage and made me take off all my clothes to see if I was wearing a wire or not. That sick bastard touched me everywhere he shouldn't have, and I wanted to spit in his face, but I swallowed my pride. Then before I left, he told me that if you even thought about talking to the police that your family would be in danger. All I could do was cry because it felt like he was so untouchable. I don't know anyone that could help us, and furthermore, I don't have the money to pay for your attorney.

I'm so sorry, Airstead. I hope that you can forgive me, but I really tried. The last thing that I wanted to do was to let you down.

Airstead crumpled the letter into a fist. His anger rushed through his veins like a fire does a forest. Trinidad was the last person that he expected to go sour on him. This game in which he was involved was now becoming a diabolical charade full of betrayal. On that very day, he vowed to repay his adversaries by defeating them in this brutal and strategic game of chess.

CHAPTER 13

THE DAY BEFORE AIRSTEAD WAS due in court, he jogged the perimeter of the gym. He found that running was the only way to relax at night. His sleep was full of gruesome nightmares that caused him to wake up in cold sweats from time to time. His public defender—an older woman named Latisha Frederick—had visited him and had promised a lighter sentence because he was a first-time offender. Irene vowed that she would stand in his corner no matter the length of his jail term.

He was beat after his tenth lap and sat down on a bench near the wall. He reached into his pants pocket and pulled out a photo of his two sons and smiled at how much they looked like him. He got to his feet and headed into the bathroom and briefly stopped at the mirror.

"You're still one handsome motherfucker." He laughed, then headed over to the urinal. Moments later, a Mexican man wearing a blue bandana and dark sunglasses entered and stood at the urinal next to him. They made eye contact.

"What's up, amigo?"

"Do I know you?"

The man smiled, then turned toward Airstead and began pissing onto his shoes. Airstead shoved him backward ruthlessly.

"What the fuck is your problem?"

The man reached under his shirt and pulled out a six-inch prison shank. "I'm going to cut your ass into little pieces, my friend."

Airstead took off his shirt and wrapped it around his forearm. They circled one another briefly, then the man lunged at him. "This is for Trinidad."

Airstead pivoted and grabbed his wrist. They tussled over to the sink and then to the window. Airstead twisted his enemy's wrist, and in one motion, shoved the shank into his stomach, then broke off the handle, making it impossible for him to retrieve the weapon from his body. He fell to his knees and grabbed Airstead's shirt. On the way down, blood flowed from his mouth, and he pawed at his abdomen.

This was Airstead's first kill, but the sight of the dying man brought a smile to his face. Maybe it was the thought of revenge or the hitman's failure, but whatever it was, it felt good.

"Tell Trinidad he failed." Then he left the room.

CHAPTER 14

AIRSTEAD ENTERED THE COURTROOM THE next morning full of anxiety. His adrenaline raced like invisible atoms. He made brief eye contact with Irene. She winked and crossed her fingers. His attorney, Latisha, was an attractive older woman who carried herself with dignity and pride.

"How are you this morning, Airstead?" She extended her hand, and they shook.

"I'm okay. Just a little nervous, that's all."

"Well, just take a seat at the table and relax. From my understanding, the judge will be out shortly, but I need to go over and have a quick word with the district attorney." She turned and walked over to the older man with the thick eyeglasses. Airstead looked on as to two attorneys talked for what seemed like forever.

When Latisha returned, she was carrying a blue sheet of paper. She took a seat, then leaned over to her client.

"Here is what the DA has for you: seeing that this is your first offense, he is willing to give you five years flat time with the possibility of early parole with good behavior."

"Is that the lowest that he could go?"

Latisha nodded. "Considering you got caught with two keys of coke and a loaded handgun, five years is one hell of a deal."

Airstead took a deep breath. "Okay, I'll take it."

"Okay. Sign right here." She pointed to the paper.

The bailiff entered the room. "All rise. The Honorable Judge Ruth Shaftner presiding."

The judge entered the room and took a seat. "This court is now in session. Please take your seats." Shaftner reviewed some papers over the rim of her glasses. "Counsel Frederick and District Attorney

Foster, it has been brought to my attention that there is a plea bargain on the table for this case. Is that correct?"

"That is correct, Your Honor. May we approach?"

"Sure, let's see what you have."

The judge and the two lawyers conversed among themselves. Airstead made eye contact with Irene. Her expression was serious, and he couldn't help but think that at any moment she would burst into tears.

"Mr. Gaddafi, would you please approach the bench."

The sound of the judge's voice made him almost sick to his stomach. He got to his feet, walked over, and stood next to Latisha.

"Your attorney, Ms. Frederick, and DA Foster have agreed to the terms of this plea and have informed you that you have the opportunity to withdraw this plea and have a jury of twelve to decide your fate. Or we can move along with the sentencing phase of this hearing."

He thought momentarily and wondered what would happen if he decided to take this case to trial. The answer was a reality check that he couldn't afford to cash. He had been caught red-handed with a gun and drugs.

"I wish to proceed, Your Honor," he spoke clearly.

"Very well, then, Mr. Gaddafi. On this day, the court has accepted your plea of guilty on the charges of drug possession and carrying an unlawful firearm. Your sentence will be five years minimum security at Acadia State Prison." She slammed the gavel with an aggressive passion.

It was all over, finally, and Airstead was coming to terms with the fact that he would probably be spending the next years of his life working as a janitor for twenty cents an hour. The bailiff placed him in cuffs, headed toward the courtroom exit, then stopped near where Irene was seated.

"Say goodbye to your girlfriend, son, because you're going to be gone for a while."

Irene got to her feet; tears were running down her face, and there was pain in her eyes that a blind man could see. She tossed her arms around his neck and kissed him with passion on his lips.

"I love you, Airstead," she whispered in his ear.

As he left the courtroom, he wondered what had just happened with Irene, but then he quickly came to terms with the fact that she had fallen in love with him. And somewhere in his heart, he felt the same.

CHAPTER 15

THE DAY THAT AIRSTEAD AWAITED had finally come. He had been in prison now for two years, and the time was picking up steam. He and Shortman kept in contact despite being in different prisons. Shortman had received seven years for his robbery charge and was getting closer to his date as well. But today, Irene was bringing his sons to see him, and he couldn't wait. He had gotten up early that morning, worked out, showered, and dressed. When he was finally called for his visit, it was almost noon. Sweat formed in his palms as the anxiety took over his body. Some of his prison friends shouted things at him as he passed the cellblock.

He entered the visiting room, wearing a smile. Contact visits were what every inmate looked forward to. He walked over to the officer's station and handed him his prison ID, then took a seat. He scanned the area and wondered what was going through the minds of the other convicts. Prison was a one-way glass family, and friends always spoke about how much they understood the pain of a captive man. But one could never know the horrors that befell the lonely one but the bleeding heart itself.

The visiting room door opened, and in walked Irene carrying two beautiful twin boys. They were more adorable now that he was seeing them in person. Two years could really change a person. Irene's hair had grown down to her lower back. She was more beautiful than the photos that she had sent. As he got to his feet, she handed him the babies. His heart turned into mush, and tears formed in his eyes as he held his sons for the first time. Irene caressed his face and kissed him with passion.

"It's been a long time, Airstead. You should've let me come a long time ago."

"I know, Irene, but I've been just trying to deal with this alone." They sat down.

"What did I tell you when you first fell? I promised to hold you no matter how long, right? So don't fault a woman for keeping her promise." She smiled.

"I'm sorry, Irene. I've just seen too many people lose their minds over females while doing time, and I'd be damned if I go through what I did with your sister. Speaking of which, how is she doing?"

One of the babies started to cry. Airstead bounced his leg. "Don't cry, Aldolphus. Daddy is right here."

Irene laughed. "That's not Aldolphus. That's Amias, the oldest."

She got to her feet and reached for the screaming child. "I can't tell them apart. How could you?"

She held the baby's hand toward him. "Amias has a beauty mark on his hand. Aldolphus doesn't."

Airstead smiled. "I will remember that for the next time."

"I don't know if there is going to be a next time," she responded.

"What do you mean?"

Irene took a deep breath. "Well, Sofia, Clevio, and I got into this big fight about you. She feared that I had been bringing the boys to see you all along and told me to find my own apartment and to stay away from the kids. She doesn't want them to know that you're their father. She has changed so much. I mean, every other day there is some guy named Sonny knocking on the door claiming that her and Clevio owe him money, and the strangest thing about it is that he works for that Trinidad guy. Now if that's not bad news, then I don't know what is."

Airstead sat silent for a moment, trying to see the logic. He looked at his two children. "Is she really that determined to keep me away from my family?"

Irene gave a look of sympathy. "We will find a way around it, baby. Just be strong."

"Photos! Get your photos taken now!" yelled an inmate with a camera.

"Why don't you and the boys take a photo together?" she suggested.

139

Airstead smiled, got to his feet, took the other baby from Irene's arms, and walked over to where the photo curtain was.

"Take a picture of me and my sons," he said to the photographer. He held one child in each arm and smiled. The man snapped the picture and the flash from it seemed to bring everything into reality.

CHAPTER 16

ICE COULDN'T FIGHT BACK HIS tears as he looked down on the man who he thought to be just a friend and a caretaker. Airstead was his father; Irene, his aunt. And he had a missing twin brother that he couldn't remember.

"What happened to my brother?"

Airstead took a deep breath, closed his eyes, then opened them again. "Your brother had cancer just like me, and he passed shortly after you guys came to see me. I wanted to tell you this years ago, but I just couldn't. I finally had you with me and didn't want to lose you or confuse you. You're my baby boy." Tears ran down the dying man's face.

"How could you do this to me, Dad?"

"I'm sorry, son. I regret not telling you more than anything in my life. Just tell me that you forgive me, son, please." His voice was weak and just above a whisper.

Ice grabbed his father's hand and kissed it gently. "I forgive you, Dad."

Airstead forced a smile. "Thank you, Ice. Thank you so much. Now I can finally rest. Leave me now, my son." His voice even weaker.

Ice leaned forward and kissed his cheek. "I love you, Dad." He turned and headed toward the door.

Airstead had lived to see his only living child grow into adulthood. He looked at his son. "I love you too," he whispered, then slowly pulled the oxygen from his nose.

With the last bit of strength that he had, he pulled the IV from his arm. Ice heard the flatline as he entered the hall. He turned on his heel and rushed back into Airstead's room, but it was too late. He had released his soul from its shell, sending it up to knock on heaven's door, and hoping that God would answer.

CHAPTER 17

ICE WAS EXHAUSTED AND WORN by sorrowful times as he walked into the house. For twenty-one years of his life, he had lived with a thousand sugarcoated lies. He took a seat on the couch without even turning on a light. The house was quiet and motionless, leading him to conclude that Irene had already been called to the hospital. He pulled out a bag of powder, dumped a large amount onto the back of his hand, and snorted it quickly. He rested his head on a pillow and closed his eyes.

When he was eleven years old, Sofia had told him a story: a twisted tale of true friendship and division by betrayal. For so long he had wondered why he never felt close to the man named Clevio and how he adored the notorious and feared man named Airstead, and now that the feelings were a reality, he was angered by their revelation. Now he understood why Sofia and Irene looked so much alike: they were sisters.

The door opened and in walked Irene. Ice sat and glared at her silhouette. She turned on the light, then grabbed herself in the bosom, astonished.

"You scared me. I didn't know you were home."

Her face was tear streaked and empty. Ice felt the fire of betrayal flowing through his veins. He jumped to his feet and lunged at her, grabbing her shoulders and forcing her into the wall.

"How could you deceive me the way that you have? We are fucking family. How could you do this to me?" He shook her little body like a rag doll, and she began to sob. "Say something!" He insisted, as his own tears began to fall.

"Aldolphus, please, I've always loved you. I never intended to hurt you. Lord knows that. How was I to go against your father? I changed your shitty diapers for God's sake. The last thing that we wanted to do was lose you or leave with more confusion than you had when you came back to us." She covered her face, then slid down the wall to the floor; her body trembled from the sobs of pain.

Ice looked down at the brokenhearted woman, then knelt and caressed her tightly in his arms. The rain began to fall outside as if God were crying his own tears of sadness as he looked down on the two lost and confused souls.

CHAPTER 18

THE TENT INSIDE THE CEMETERY was filled with friends and associates of the late Airstead Gaddafi. The late afternoon clouds moved by gracefully, indicating that darkness would be approaching fast. Ice hugged Irene tightly to prevent her constant trembling; all the while he masked his own pain with sunglasses. Shortman sat beside Kaila; his face was in his palms, mourning the loss of his only best friend. All were quiet while the minister read Bible verses and talked about the hope of a heavenly resurrection. He talked for what seemed like forever, then encouraged the mourning family to join him in prayer.

After the ceremony, Ice headed toward his car.

"Hey, Ice, wait a second." He turned and looked into the bloodshot eyes of Shortman. "I'm going to take Irene home. I know you probably want to be alone, so I figured I would take the responsibility off your hands."

Ice smirked weakly. "Thanks, Shorty, no problem." The two men embraced momentarily.

"Don't ever doubt the fact that I would have died for your father." Ice could hear the intensity in his voice and could feel that this man had truly been a friend to his father.

"I know, Shorty. Believe me, I do."

He turned on his heel and got into the car, then briefly looked at the crowd of people still mingling under the tent. Well over five hundred, he estimated, and wondered who they all were. He pulled out a bag of powder and snorted some up quickly, then reclined his head and closed his eyes. The world was his now: the casino and all the property his father had owned.

His train of thought was derailed by a knocking on his window. He opened his eyes and saw a woman holding a sleeping baby. She was beautiful; her hair was long and jet-black; and her eyes were a precious marble green that complemented her light skin. It had been since right after high school that he had laid eyes on her, but suddenly an overwhelming feeling of love entered his heart. She was once upon a time the epitome of his dreams; then she became the unfinished chapter in his life. Tracey Spencer, his one true love.

He unlocked the door as she made her way over to the passenger side and got into the car. The child that she held in her arms rested peacefully on her shoulder and slept without interruption. They looked at one another and both seemed to struggle with which words had the sounds and the actions to match. On their last encounter, Tracey had said goodbye forever.

"So what brings you back here, college girl?" He broke the silence.

"I was in town visiting my grandma when I heard the news, so I thought I would at least come and pay my respects to your father. He was a good man and always treated me with love."

Ice exhaled deeply. "Well, I accept your deposit. You've paid. Now what?" His tone was rude and full of resentment.

"Aldolphus, I know you must hate me for leaving you the way that I did, but please try not to use the past against me. We were in love at one time. Or did you forget about that?"

"How could I forget? Memories of you have haunted me since the day you left."

"Ice, please, do me a favor today: don't think about our bad times because I know in my heart that our good will drown them one thousand times over."

He chuckled. "You know, Tracey. That's what I felt like when you left: being drowned a thousand times over." He ran his fingers through his hair and let out a sigh. "I'm sorry, Tracey. I shouldn't be taking my personal feelings out on you. It's just that a lot has changed in my life over these past few weeks." He thought about telling Tracey about his revelation but decided that it was too much to address at the moment.

"Well, I'm staying at the Babylon Hotel. Would you be a gentleman and escort us to our room?" She rubbed the baby's head.

"I've always been a gentleman." He looked at her seductively.

She smiled. "The more things change, the more they stay the same."

He started the car, then pulled out onto Cemetery Road. "So who is the little guy?"

She smiled. "I was wondering what was taking you so long to ask that. This is Renaldo Spencer III, my pride and joy. His father was an ex-knucklehead turned college boy who I fell for trying to forget you. It didn't work out, and I left school and became a full-time mom. What can I say? Another case of being young and dumb."

Ice shook his head. "So do you have a stable place to live? You know I own property from here to LA."

"Well, I've been staying with a girlfriend of mine and working part-time at the state police barracks in the dispatch center."

Ice laughed. "So you're joining in on the war against crime now?"

She shoved him playfully. "Not exactly. It's just a job. Stop harassing me." She laughed.

The conversation continued about everything that had changed since they had last met until they reached the hotel parking lot. He turned off the engine and looked over at Tracey.

"Here you are, Ms. Spencer. Safe at your lavish motel. Courtesy of Ice's cab service." The air was empty for a moment.

"It was good seeing you again, Ice." Her voice was gentle and full of truth.

"It was nice to see you as well, Tracey. You take care of yourself."

She got out the car and headed into the building. He watched her vanish and still felt like business between them was unfinished. He turned the car around and left the lot.

Tracey waited until she reached the elevator before she let the first tear drop. Deep in her heart, she felt empty and unfulfilled. There was still a love that ached in her heart for Ice that proved to be stronger than hurricane winds. Once she entered her room, she took her child to the bedroom and laid his small body on the bed.

She entered the living room and took a seat on the couch. *Why did it still hurt so bad after all this time?* she wondered, running her fingers through her hair. She smiled as she relived yesterday's memories. She picked up the phone and ordered a bottle of wine from room service. She was in the mood to relax and reminisce about the past.

After taking a hot shower, she dressed in a cute red slip, then looked at herself in the mirror. *You haven't lost your sex appeal yet, darling.* She blew herself a kiss and laughed at her own silly behavior. She put her long hair into a ponytail, then headed back into the living room.

There was a knock at the door. "Room service for Ms. Spencer."

She put on her bathrobe, took off the security chain, and snatched open the door. The sight of Ice standing there was like an angel that had crossed over from her dreams. He held a bottle in his hand and wore a smile on his face that Tracey could never resist.

"I think that you forgot to pay your cab fare."

She pulled him into the room and began to kiss him feverishly and pull off articles of clothing at the same time. He sat the bottle on the coffee table then engaged in the passion.

"Remember how it used to be?" she whispered.

Ice opened her robe, then pushed her back onto the couch. He removed his pants.

"Remember the last time I let you have control? Well, it's my turn now." He mounted her.

"Don't hurt me, baby. This pussy is so tight."

He covered her mouth, then directed the length of his manhood into her body. She let out a moan as he ran his fingers through her hair, making love to her soul.

"Do you remember this dick, baby? Do you?"

Her screams of pleasure and pain were evident. "Oh, I remember the dick well, too fucking well," she responded through clenched teeth. She grabbed a handful of his hair and pulled his face close to hers. "I love you, Ice. I've never stopped." Her terms of endearment only fueled his passion as they spent what was left of that day making love soul to soul.

Ice woke up the following morning to an empty bed.

"Tracey, Tracey," he called twice.

He got up from the sofa bed, then walked down to the bedroom. It was empty as well. Then he noticed the letter that was taped to mirror.

> Ice, there is no easy way to say goodbye to you. When I said that I loved you last night, it was the realist truth. It's just that everything is so confusing for me right now, just like I know that it is for you. Honestly, I've been confused since I last saw you. Making love to you was like knocking on heaven's door. You're the only man who I love and ever will. What we share can't be put into words, but I only can say that our castle of love is a bottomless well. I'm sorry that I left without saying goodbye, but I knew that if I did, it would be almost impossible to leave you again.
>
> Love Always,
> Tracey

He flopped down onto the bed. Life had a mysterious way of repeating old emotions. She had left him again without really saying goodbye. He shook his head and smiled weakly, for he knew that the chapter was complete and the book closed.

He pulled into the garage and turned off the engine. Something about his life appeared like a resurrected dream. Every day was a new revelation and a new encounter with yesterday.

He walked into the house and thought briefly about Eva as he grabbed the chain that she had given him. She was a woman who had loved him so dearly as a child. He felt some guilt that his lavish lifestyle had somehow caused him to forget the one person that had shined sunlight onto his shadowed heart. He entered the library and took a seat behind a desk and placed his head into his palms. There was a knock at the door, and Irene entered the room, dressed in her bathrobe. Her eyes were wet from tears. She took a seat on the old country-style sofa.

"Hey." He looked at her. "What's up to me?"

"Everything: the casino, the real estate, the seventy kilos of White Girl that your father left for you. This is your kingdom now, Ice, but it's up to you how to rule it." She paused as to let her words become gospel in his mind. She looked toward the sky. "Your father built this operation from zero, right out of prison. I remember like it was yesterday."

*   *   *   *   *

Flashback

Irene checked her watch as she waited outside the prison.

"Come on, Airstead," she said under her breath.

Fifteen minutes had expired from his release time. She had already set the meeting up with Trinidad, and if they didn't make it on time, the whole plan would go to waste. She looked in the rear-view mirror and saw him approaching. *He looked cute in his prison blues,* she thought, smiling to herself. He climbed into the passenger side.

"I thought they decided to keep you for an extra year." She kissed his lips.

"Ain't no jail in the world that can hold me past my time."

"Yeah, and if they did, I would blow up the fucking place to get you out." She laughed, starting the car and pulling out onto the road.

"So did you bring my tools?"

She smiled. "Look under your seat."

He reached under and revealed a black backpack and looked inside, then smiled devilishly.

"That was the best that I could do," she said, waiting for his approval.

"You did one hell of a job." He examined the two .357 Magnums, then pulled the box of bullets from the bag. "Hmmm, hollow tips: good choice for a woman with no real dark side." He chuckled.

"I received a letter from your friend Shortman last week, and he said that they might let him go early to a halfway house on good behavior." She changed the subject.

"Oh really? Well, I hope that he does because by then I should be rollin' big-time."

Trinidad pulled onto the dirt road and checked the time. "Airstead should be arriving any minute now, and all you have to do, Valley, is watch his every move. If he even looks funny, blow his fucking top off." He looked over at his passenger.

"I got it, boss, but I don't think he is going to try anything. He has no idea that you put that jailhouse hit on him."

"Yeah, I guess you're right, Valley. I gave Caesar specific instructions not to mention names, so I'm sure that he toed the line carefully. We will just see how he acts when he gets here."

At that very moment, the car pulled in behind them. Airstead looked at Irene. "When the gunfire starts, just lie on the seat. I'm going to hit this chump, take the coke, and we out like the trash on a Thursday."

He got out of the car at the same time as Trinidad and Valley. The scene almost seemed to happen in slow motion. Airstead smiled as he walked toward them.

"It's been a long time, Airstead. We missed you." The words echoed, it seemed. Airstead reached under his shirt and pulled out the two pistols and began squeezing. Trinidad grabbed Valley and used him as a shield. He never had a chance to reach because the burning lead had already scorched the life from his body. Trinidad returned fire, and a bullet grazed Airstead's shoulder, but he was determined to win this smoke pole shootout. Trinidad ran out of bullets, then turned and tried to run but couldn't move at the light speed of the bullet of revenge; it struck him in the back of the head and exploded his face into a bleeding open hole. Airstead popped the trunk of the car and took the sixteen kilos of powder and a duffle bag filled with money.

"And the rest is history."

* * * * *

Irene got to her feet. "I just wanted to let you know how hard we worked to build this thing of ours. I will be behind you 100 percent, but you have to be strong and willing to play by the blood rules." She walked away. He sat and let her words soak in.

His father had fought to get to the top, and now he had to figure out how to stay there. Things would be different now that he was in charge. He would organize a gang of heartless shooters that would die like a suicide bomber for the family. He realized the realness of this game of death. His father had left a war going on, and he was the chosen soldier to fight on the front lines.

He walked out of the room and into the kitchen where Irene sat, drinking a cup of coffee.

"Call Shortman and have him and security detail meet me at the other house in a few hours, and any of my father's old connects." He kissed her cheek, then left the house before she could respond.

He climbed behind the wheel. It had been years since he had seen Eva and had decided not to wait another second. He pulled out a bag of powder and snorted some. He never thought that at such a young age, he would be so powerful. Irene's speech meant a lot to him, but keeping his father's dream meant more. It was late afternoon when he pulled into the lot of Saint Joseph's Hospital. The breeze was slightly comforting as he got out of the car and headed toward the entrance. He gripped his chain and said a silent prayer before walking through the glass doors.

As he approached the service station, an attractive blond with a friendly smile greeted him. "How are you, sir? Welcome to Saint Joseph's. How can we be of any assistance?"

He smiled as he realized that the greeting was rehearsed and used often. "I'm here to meet with Mr. Roberts."

She gave an inquisitive look. "Are you a friend or family of Mr. Roberts?"

"Something like that. Let's just say that he knew me when I was a child." She smiled then picked up the phone at her station and dialed a three-digit number.

Ice drank in more of the scene as she talked on the phone. He felt like a kid again, like the day that Eva had given him the necklace and the gentle words that she uttered. *With this, we will always be together, and whenever you have a problem, hold on to it tightly and pray to God, and he will answer your prayers.*

"Sir, pardon me, sir."

He snapped back to reality. "I'm sorry. I was somewhere else."

"It's fine. I just don't believe that I caught your name." She held her hand over the phone.

"Jackson, Aldolphus Jackson," he responded.

She spoke briefly, then hung up the phone. "Mr. Roberts will see you now. Just take the elevator up to the fourth floor, and his office is the first one on the left."

"Thanks, beautiful." She blushed as he headed down the hall.

Seeing Eva would probably change his whole life. She might even be able to make him feel guilty about his new life choice. It didn't matter, he reasoned, as long as he got the opportunity to tell her how much he really cared for her. The elevator opened, and the butterflies began to flutter. He walked up to the closed door and tapped on it gently.

"Come in." The voice was smooth and well guided. He opened the door. Roberts hadn't changed much at all: in fact, he looked exactly the same except for the thick glasses he sported.

"How are you, Aldolphus? It's been a long time!" They shook hands.

"It's been years—over ten. I thought you might have forgotten me by now."

"I'm old, son, not senile. I remembered you better than most, especially that little move you and Tank pulled at the facility." He laughed.

Ice smirked. "Well, I'm glad that you remember me."

"So what can I do for you, son?"

Ice took a deep breath. "I'm here to see Eva. I know it's been a long time, but it's better late than never."

Roberts's skin turned pale. "Excuse me for a second." He got up and left the room. Ice sat and waited for what seemed like an eternity, then the door opened and in walked a short woman wearing a white nurse's uniform. Her beauty was that of a young princess: her skin was honey coated, her eyes were a deep dark brown, and her hair a matching shade. She walked softly with the grace of a panther and took a seat behind Roberts's desk. They made eye contact, and it appeared that they both were trying to hypnotize the other with the intensity of the stare.

"I take it that you're the young man searching for Eva." Her voice was gentle.

"Yes, that's correct." She sighed, then ran her perfectly manicured nails through her hair. "I'm sorry to inform you that Eva passed away three years ago from a massive heart attack. She was buried at Trinity Cemetery a few miles down the road."

The words cut through Ice like a sword. He bowed his head in defeat, then looked back up into the tear-soaked eyes of the young lady. "How did you know Eva?" she questioned.

"Well, I was crippled from a car accident for a short time, and she was the woman who nursed me back to health during my darkest hour. I just wish I had come earlier." He got to his feet. "Thanks for your help, Miss—"

"Lawson, Indeshea Lawson." She got to her feet and extended her hand. Like a true gentleman, he caressed hers like it had a sign that read Fragile. "I know better than anyone how you must feel. Eva was my grandmother." A tear traveled down her cheek. She walked around the desk and pulled him close to her, resting her head on his chest. He was caught off guard but also understood her pain so embraced her. Abruptly, she pushed him away. "I'm so sorry. I just lost all control of my emotions." She covered her mouth.

"There is no need for an apology. I totally understand." He turned and headed for the door, then reached into his pocket and pulled out a business card and handed it to her. "I'm having a party on Saturday night. I hope to hear from you or see you there." He left the room. Indeshea wiped her flushed cheeks, then studied the card closely and gave a smirk.

Ice walked through the cemetery, feeling the pains of lost loves clouding his heart. He approached Eva's headstone, knelt, then grabbed his necklace. His conversation was held with God and far beyond human understanding.

CHAPTER 19

HE ENTERED THE LIBRARY AND stood at the head of the table. He met eyes with Shortman, who was seated at the opposite end. They smiled. Irene entered and took her position next to her nephew. He allowed his gaze to fall upon all in attendance before the carefully prepared words started to flow: "The reason that I called this meeting is because you were employed by my father before his passing, and now that he has left us, I plan to continue running his business and continue its growth, with the addition of some new innovative ideas and hostile takeovers." He paused. "Everyone will carry firearms, and those of you that don't know how to use a tool will be taught to do so by Shortman." He turned his attention to the two husky men at the table. "Rock: you and Buddy will be responsible for delivering our product to the street team and other clients. John: you and Falcon will be responsible for picking up the shipments coming in from our Hungarian connect on Fridays. And Spartan: you know your job, but I'm also hiring you to obtain as many high-powered weapons as you can. Meaning grenades, rocket launchers, assault rifles, and whatever else that you can get your hands on. As for Kaila: you and the other girls will keep your same jobs until I inform you of other plans."

He scanned the room, studying each person carefully. "If anyone disagrees with how I plan to run things, you are free to go." He pointed at the door. No one moved or even shifted in their chairs.

That day was the birth of a new organization: a unified gang that would learn that loyalty could turn lethal when you're willing to play the game of death.

Gaddafi's Palace was in full swing as Indeshea entered the building. It was so crowded that she thought about turning and walking out of the door.

"Are you looking for me?" The baritone in her ear made her flinch, and she was caught off guard, forcing her to turn aggressively. Ice laughed and held his hands up to surrender. "Hold up, little lady. I ain't going to bite."

She laughed. "I'm sorry. You just startled me, that's all."

"Well, I am truly sorry, Miss Lady. Can I be a gentleman and buy you a drink?" He took her by the hand and escorted her into the club area.

Kaila approached. "What can I get for you, boss?"

He looked at Indeshea. "I will have whatever the queen is having."

She felt herself blush. "A club soda will be enough for me, thanks."

Kaila laughed. "Two club sodas coming right up." She walked away.

"Let's take a seat." He walked her to a booth that was kind of set by itself.

"So what exactly do you do for a living?" She admired the scene.

"You're looking at it: I'm a mogul and a casino owner."

She chuckled. "I hope you don't think that I just came off the porch: I'm sure that your money is dirtier than the government's."

He laughed. "Maybe it is, and it matters to who?"

She sucked her teeth. "It surely doesn't matter to me. Whatever you're doing has been going on long before you met me."

"That's true. But you say that as if we had met under different circumstances that things would be different."

She smiled, showing her perfect teeth. "You read deeper than what's written, Mr. Ice." Her tone was sarcastic.

Kaila brought their drinks, and Ice took a sip immediately. "You know, Indeshea. I admire a woman who challenges me and attempts to compete."

"Oh, you do? And why is that, mister?"

"Because I get better pleasure when they submit."

She took a sip of her drink and gave a sexy look. "So you think that you can make me submit?"

He gave a diabolical smile. "No disrespect intended, but I could make your mother scream."

She laughed hard. "I wonder what I'm getting myself into."

"Nothing bad, Indeshea. You're about to be painted by the brush of a sexual artist."

Irene approached and kissed his cheek. "Hey, handsome." She took a seat. "Who's your friend?" She studied the younger woman closely.

"Oh, I'm sorry. Indeshea, this is my aunt, Irene." They shook hands.

Falcon approached the table. He was a six-foot-nine brown-skinned man. "Boss, we have a problem in the casino area. There is some character trying to get into the party without an invitation and insists that you and him are good friends, but I've never saw the cat before."

Ice frowned. "Did he give you a name?"

"No, he just said he wanted to speak directly to you."

Ice got to his feet. "Are you going to be okay waiting here, Deshea?"

Before she could respond, Irene had already started speaking. "Do you need to ask if she's with me?" He smiled and turned on his heel.

"So what do you think of my nephew?"

Indeshea smiled as they both watched him walking away. "Charming. Absolutely charming."

Ice walked into the lobby and saw a tall dark-complexioned man talking to his security. He had broad, muscular shoulders and a shaved head. They made eye contact, and Ice nearly melted as they approached one another.

"One for one, one for all," he said.

"Back to back until God finds a way for a true soldier." Ice finished. The men embraced. "It's been a long time, Tank. I thought I would never see you again."

"I thought the same, until I read about Airstead in the paper. I read a few lines further and whose name did I see. None other than the notorious Aldolphus Jackson." He laughed.

"Shhh, don't say that name too loud. They call me Ice now." The old friends shared a laugh. "Let's go to my office. We have a lot to catch up on." He put his arm around the more muscular man, and they headed into the back of the building. Once in the office, they both sat down.

"So how is your mama doing?"

Tank shook his head. "Man, she done lost her rabbit-ass mind trippin' on pops, so now they keeping her locked up in a crazy house. I used to visit her before I went to the state pen."

Ice frowned. "You've been to the pen?"

"Hell yeah, my nigga. I just got out two weeks ago."

"Damn, Tank, what kinda shit have you been into?"

Tank took a deep breath. "Man, it's a crazy story."

Ice looked down at his diamond Rolex. "We ain't got nothing but time, bay bro."

"Well, I fucked around and married Summer when we turned eighteen. She was pregnant with my second daughter and money was tight, so I started this armed robbery shit. Things was like butter for a minute, but Summer was never satisfied." He paused and looked Ice in the eye. "So I went for the big leagues and pulled off a bank job and ended up doing three to six up in Chino."

Ice shook his head. "So what's the situation with you and her now?"

Tank laughed. "You know how that shit goes. The game never changes, only the playas. If you ain't there to scratch that pussy, then somebody will. That sorry bitch don't even know that I'm home."

"Do you have a place to stay?"

"Yeah, me and a couple of cats that I was locked with got a place in my old projects."

Ice shook his head. "Check this out: I have a four-bedroom house connected to one of my places. You're more than welcome to stay there if interested."

Tank glowed with excitement. "I'm more than interested, but I can't bail out on my comrades like that because me and these dudes have been through some shit together in the slammer, and besides that, these dudes can probably help you out with your street pharmacy business." His look was serious and full of meaning.

Ice chuckled. "Thanks, but no thanks, Tank. I have too much help as it is."

"Hold up, Aldolphus. Hear me out before you shoot me down. My friends are chemists." There was a pause.

"Yeah, and so what in the fuck is that supposed to mean to me?"

Tank leaned forward in his chair. "These dudes have made a new drug that is cocaine-based but five times stronger than your typical shit."

"So why ain't they rich yet if they have this wonder drug on the streets?"

Tank sighed. "Because they don't have a large enough supply to get the streets hopping. That's where you come in."

Ice frowned. "Hold up. Let me get this straight, Tank. I know you're not asking me to put my shit on the line for two dudes in a jack-in-the-box that I don't know?"

"I'm glad that you said that because I brought some proof."

Tank reached into his pocket and revealed a capsule filled with a blue powder and handed it to Ice. "Welcome to the new world order, my friend. Get one of these flunkies to test this shit out, and if it's not what I say it is, then I will never bring it up again."

Ice smiled. "If I'm going to put my product on the line, I might as well test it myself." He dumped some of the powder on the back of his hand and snorted it up quickly. Tank studied his friend closely. Ice shook his head back and forth as the powder gave him an intense feeling of euphoria, almost like a dream. "Wow. What the fuck is this shit?" He laughed, still trying to get focused.

"It's the Blue Monster, baby boy. Too much of this shit will literally kill you dead."

Ice held the capsule up to the light. "We could control the world with this shit."

Tank smiled. "That's what I was trying to tell you from jump."

Aldolphus smiled at his long-lost friend. "Let's do this: I will send a car to pick your friends up. We can start negotiations as early as tomorrow."

"Sounds good to me, but there is one thing that I left out about my friends: they are twin brothers from India, and only one of them can speak English."

"That's cool. As long as they can communicate among themselves without error, then they are as good as gold." They both laughed. "Come on, let's celebrate."

A city known as a gangster's dream and a player's fantasy; a city that holds a haunted gridlock on the youth; a place of beauty and death. Two childhood friends reunited with the sole purpose to rule the city with the fist of Thor. But the game of blood rules is dangerous for all those that gamble at the devil's roulette table.

Ice woke up the following morning and looked into the beautiful sleeping face of Indeshea. The night had been long and passionate for both of them, and he knew that she wouldn't soon forget him. He checked his watch, and it read 9:00 a.m. He still had four and a half hours before Tank would be arriving at the casino with his friends. He took a quick shower, then dressed carefully, as always, then wrote a note to Deshea. Afterward, he headed down the steps where Shortman was waiting at the door.

"Are you ready, boss?"

"As ready as I ever will be."

They got into Shortman's Lincoln. As they pulled onto the street, Ice pulled out a capsule filled with the blue powder and snorted it.

"Do you want to try some of this?" He held it toward Shortman.

"Nah, man, I'll stick to the white snow." He laughed.

"Man, once you try some of this shit, you ain't going to want anything else. This shit is going to rule the world and make a lot of enemies. You mark my words: in three months, I will be sitting on top of the blue mountain." He laughed.

They talked more about the new drug until they reached the casino. By the time Tank and his friends arrived, Ice and Shortman were seated in the back office waiting patiently. Suddenly there was a knock at the door, and Falcon entered the room.

"They have arrived, sir."

"Okay, send them in," he responded.

Tank entered the room, followed closely by two bronze-complexioned Indian men. They both had short haircuts and large hooked noses. Though they were identical twins, only one of them had glasses. Tank and Ice embraced.

"These are my friends that I told you about: Raul and Raffon."

Ice extended his hand and shook with both men before taking a seat. Tank looked at Raul—the one with the glasses and the only English-speaking one of the two.

"The floor is yours, Raul." He pushed his rims up on his nose, pulled a writing tablet from his bag, and cleared his throat.

"Me and my brother have a new powder that is created from a cocaine base but has the power to comatose and even kill if abused by the user. Our process raises the potency nearly five times the natural chemical strength. The only downfall is that we don't have enough powder to work with, nor do we have the lab space to produce like we can, not to mention a few other ingredients needed to bring the future of drug dealing to life."

Ice smiled, nodding and indicating that he was impressed by the man's intellect. "Let me take a look at the formula."

There was an uncomfortable silence. Raul looked at his brother, and they spoke briefly in their own language. "I'm sorry, sir. No one can have the formula but us. You see, if we give you the formula, you could always hire other lab techs to perform the process and then you could dispose of us."

Ice smiled. "Listen, Raul: I'm putting my father's life's work on the line. You guys need me. I don't need you. I'm already rich. I just think it's safer for me to know where my product is going. I will save it on a disk, then you can get rid of that paper trail that you've been carrying around."

Raul looked at Tank. "Trust him, Raul. He's telling you the truth."

Raul turned and spoke with his brother again, then without further delay, tore the sheet of paper off the tablet and handed it to Ice. Ice studied it for a few moments before he started typing.

"What's the name of this drug anyway?" he asked, looking up from his computer.

Raul laughed. "We don't have a name for it, sir."

"Good. We do now."

He continued to type. After he finished, he removed the disk from the drive and locked it in his desk. He looked around the room at all its occupants. "Today's the birth date of the new street drug called Raw Ice."

Tank nodded. "I like that, Raw Ice. It sounds strong, just like us."

Ice picked the globe up off his desk. "The world is mine."

BOOK 3

Revelations

CHAPTER 1

THREE MONTHS LATER, JAKARTA KENICHI, the leader of the Yamaguchi-Gumi Japanese mafia, was reading the newspaper. The bold letters caught his attention: "New Drug Called Ice, Trumping the Street Value of Cocaine." He tossed the paper to the floor.

"Yana, Yana!" he yelled.

A young man in his early twenties entered the room and bowed his head in respect. "Yes, Father, what is it?"

Jakarta got up from his desk and walked over to the large window overlooking the city. "I want you and Nara to sweep this whole damn city until you find out who is responsible for producing this new shit called Raw Ice. And when you do, make them an offer to buy the formula so we can start supplying our own people. We have already lost about $3 million in sales because of this shit. Before you know it, we will be totally out of business."

Yana listened to his father's instructions. "It will be done, Father." He turned and left the room.

Ice pulled into the lot of Saint Joseph's and waited for Indeshea to exit the building. She had become a very important part of his life over the past few months. He couldn't wait to see her; she had called him earlier and told him that she had something urgent to discuss with him. His anxiety peaked as she got into the car and the butterflies in his stomach did what they do best: flutter.

"I put the Vegas mansion up for sale today. I figured since we have been spending most of our time out here at the smaller mansion, we really don't need that one any longer." He looked over at his girlfriend. "What's with the long face?"

"I'm just tired, that's all. I had a long day."

"So long that you can't tell me what was so urgent earlier?"

"Can we talk about it later? Right now, I just want to sleep." She relaxed in her seat and closed her eyes. He smiled and pulled onto the street. Women are sensitive and special creatures, and it takes a real man to understand them.

Ice sank into his own thoughts. He was living his father's dream. Raw Ice was becoming the fastest-selling street drug in history, and knowing that it was his money and product that made it happen brought a smile to his face.

He and Tank were supplying half of the city, and the $3 million a month that he was collecting was the smoking gun of evidence. He was becoming a legend in his own time; his reality was the dreams of others, and his nightmares were their reality. He felt that his father was guiding him and in the direction of the successful.

The ride seemed shorter than normal; maybe from the tunnel that his train of thought had run through. He pulled into the garage, then shook Deshea gently.

"Wake up, babe." She opened her eyes, then stretched. "Do you feel better now?" he asked, getting out of the car and rushing to the other side to open her door.

"Aren't you just the gentleman?" Her voice was charming with a hint of sarcasm as she walked past him. Once inside, they went up to the bedroom. Deshea went into the bathroom and turned on the shower.

He took a seat on the bed, picked up the phone, and dialed a number. It rang twice, then was answered. "Shortman's Takeout. We deliver."

Ice laughed. "What's up, Shorty? Is Tank around?"

"Yeah, that nigga around, but Kaila has him tied up right now. If you know what I mean."

Ice laughed. "Okay, I will see you guys at the casino later." They hung up.

Deshea entered the room wearing a bath towel around her chest. *She was so beautiful,* he thought to himself. She walked over to the mirror and began brushing her hair. She was the kind of woman who could turn a man on with her slightest movement. He got up from the bed, walked over, stood behind her, and gently wrapped his arms around her waist. He kissed her earlobe, exhaled his hot breath onto her neck, and began to work his way downward. She let out a soft intimate moan.

"Do you like that, baby?" He removed the towel, exposing every precious curve on her body. He then picked her up, walked over to the bed, and laid her gently down on it. He removed his own shirt and pants, then crawled on top of her. They began to kiss with a slow passion. He allowed his hand to explore her body until he found the wet flesh between her legs. He loved seeing her in pleasure as her body convulsed slightly.

"I want you inside of me," she whispered. He grabbed his dick and rubbed against her clitoris. "Put it in me, please, Ice, fill me up with your love," she cooed.

"Shhh, not yet baby."

She gripped his manhood. "Fuck that. You're going to give me this dick." She forced him into her body and tossed her legs in the air and began thrusting her pelvis to meet him halfway. "Tell me, baby, how hot this pussy is for you."

Ice placed one of his hands under the small of her back. "I'm insatiable when I'm loving you, Deshea."

"Are you? Show me how much." He turned her on her stomach then spread her thighs as far as they would go without hurting her, then he entered her and began working his hips in a circular motion. "Oooh, that dick feels so good. You're gonna make me come so hard, baby."

"Come to Daddy, baby. Wet that dick up with that hot come."

She lifted and began to meet his powerful strokes. "Here it comes. Here I come, baby. All over that fat dick." The passion and ecstasy became so intense that they both climaxed and were more than fulfilled. Sweat covered their bodies, and the breathing was heavy. She looked up into her man's face.

"Ice, I'm pregnant."

Gaddafi's Palace was just heating up. Ice, Tank, Shortman, Falcon, and Buddy were seated at a round table. Tank looked over at Ice.

"Did you happen to read the newspaper today?"

"No, I didn't see it. What was it about?"

"The same thing that it's been about for three months now: Raw Ice, baby boy." Shortman interrupted.

"Yeah, and according to the papers, our shit has been wiping out the sales of regular coke by the milestones," Tank added.

Ice smiled. "A few months from now, we will have this whole damn city locked down like a prison after a riot."

Tank laughed. "Ice, I never thought that you and I would team up and rule the world together."

Ice turned his attention to Buddy, who was a short, stocky man. "Did you go by the lab today?"

He shifted his weight toward Ice. "Yeah, I went by there this morning. The twins had produced almost seventy kilos at that time."

Ice nodded. "Good job. But tomorrow I want eighty, and then the day after, ninety." He laughed.

"We have company, boys," said Tank, pulling out his weapon as six Japanese men in trench coats approached the table.

"I am Yana Kenichi, son of Jakarta. I am looking to have business with the Iceman."

"I'm the fucking Iceman," snapped Shortman, jumping to his feet and pulling his weapon. Yani and his crew showed no fear as they gave no reaction to the antics.

Ice got to his feet and spread his arms in a gesture to calm the situation. "Put your guns away, boys. I'm the Iceman that you speak of."

Yana chuckled. "I see that you have loyal soldiers, Mr. Iceman, but one of them is probably a rat hiding in your cheese hole."

"You know what, chow mein face. I don't think I like your attitude," snapped Tank, lunging toward him.

Ice pulled him backward. "Calm down, Tank. What can I help you with, Mr. Kenichi?"

"I come on behalf of my father. He is willing to pay a large sum of money for the formula that creates the superdrug known as Raw Ice."

Ice shook his head and took a seat. "I'm sorry, Mr. Kenichi. My formula is not for sale."

Yana sighed. "My father will not take kindly to this sort of news. You are putting us out of business."

Ice cleared his throat and this time spoke with more aggression, "Look, meatball, for the last time, my formula is not for sale. Do you need a translator?"

He took a sip of his drink. Yana smiled. "Very well, Iceman, You will be hearing from us soon." They turned and left the area.

Falcon looked over at Ice. "Who in the fuck is Jakarta Kenichi?"

"I don't know him personally, but he is supposed to be the don and the leader of the Yamaguchi crime family. He owns that hotel downtown," Tank answered.

"Well, fuck the Kenichi crime family. It's a new breed of gangster on these streets, and whatever route they want to take, we can go there too. I will be damned if these rice-eating bastards make me fold under pressure."

"Man, don't even trip off that shit. All those Japs know how to do is cook rice and do karate. Not even Bruce Lee could beat a bullet." Tank laughed.

Shortman looked over at him. "Bruce Lee was Chinese, not Japanese." All the men laughed.

Tank put up his middle finger. "Fuck you, you wanna be technical ass, nigga." They laughed even harder as May Ling approached.

"Can I get you guys more drinks?" Shortman reached up and pulled her down next to him. "When can I get some more of that chow mein on my dick?" She laughed and got to her feet.

"No chow mein while I'm on the clock. Do you guys want drinks or not?"

"Yeah, get us a round of Hennessy," responded Ice. She walked away.

"Is it true that those Jap bitches got slanted pussies?" asked Tank, looking at Shortman, who started laughing right away.

"Man, I ain't even going to lie to you, bro. I be so busy digging her garden up that I can't even remember the shape of the peaches. Can you dig it, soul brother? But believe me. The next time, I will be checking just for you, my nigga." They slapped hands.

Yana and his goons entered Jakarta's office. He was seated on a couch, watching his big-screen television. They all bowed their heads before Yana spoke. "Father, I have some bad news: the Iceman refuses to comply with your request."

Jakarta got to his feet. "Just who is this Iceman that you speak of?"

"He owns the casino Gaddafi's Palace. Father, we told him that you wished to conduct business, and he said that he would not be interested in selling his formula to us."

Jakarta chuckled. "I will contact the Iceman myself, and if he refuses, we start whipping out his soldiers one by one until he hands it over."

"Man, I have a strange feeling about that Yana dude with all that Jakarta talk," Ice said, looking over at Tank, who was seated on the passenger side of the car. He pulled into the garage.

"Don't worry about that dude. He ain't gonna do nothing but beg like his bitch-ass son did tonight."

Ice looked ahead for a second and appeared to be in a trance. "Tank, promise something." His voice was full of meaning and depth.

"Anything for you, Ice. You're my brother."

"Promise me that if anything happens to me that you will watch over Deshea and my child."

Tank studied him closely. "If you die, then I die, but if you live, then so will I."

Ice looked at his best friend. "I love you, Tank."

"I love you, too, bro." The two men got out of the car and went their separate ways.

Ice entered the house and saw that Irene was on the couch. "Hey, handsome, how was your night?"

"Draining for sure."

"Raul called earlier. He said that he needs to see you at the lab tomorrow about more supplies. He also said that they love the flat that you gave them to stay in."

He nodded. "Okay, sounds good. Where's Deshea?"

"She went up to the west wing about an hour ago. She wasn't feeling well. You know how pregnant life is."

Ice laughed. "I don't. I've never been pregnant before." He headed up the stairs and entered the bedroom. Deshea was seated on the bed with tears coming down her cheek. "What's wrong, baby?" He sat next to her and caressed her face between his palms.

She slapped them away. "Everything is the fuck wrong!" She got to her feet.

"Deshea, calm down and tell me what the fuck you're talking about."

"Listen to your fucking answering machine," she cried. He walked over and pushed the button. It started with heavy breathing and then the eerie voice spoke.

"Hello, Iceman, I'm sure you know who this is. I'm very disappointed in you for not accepting my offer. Now, you have twenty-four hours to reconsider before people will start to disappear, and don't think about running because I have my eye on you. Ha ha ha." The laugh was diabolical. Ice picked up the machine and slammed it to the floor.

"Ice, I'm so afraid."

"I know, baby. I know." He walked over and held her tightly. "No one is going to hurt my family, I promise."

That night, sleep was hard to catch up with, as nightmares kept waking him up.

He was in a cemetery and the air was cold and wet. The cries of the owls rang like thunderclaps in his head.

Suddenly, a voice whispered in his ear, "Leave the people. You're alone. Fight alone and die alone. Leave the people before it's too late."

Then, out of the mist, a little boy appeared. "Daddy, don't let the monster get me, please, Daddy," he cried.

Ice sat up in the bed covered in sweat; his heart fighting to explode from his body. He ran his fingers through his hair and looked over at his sleeping girlfriend. He kissed her stomach, then jumped into the shower.

After getting dressed, he dialed a number. It rang four times before a woman answered.

"Hello?"

"What's up, Kaila. This is Ice. Is Tank around?"

"Yeah, he is right here."

"What's up, Ice?" His voice was tired and husky.

"Boy, you need to stay your ass out of the pussy and get focused."
He laughed.

"I'm always on point, baby boy, but the pussy is good. I can't
even lie about that."

"Well, I'm getting ready to go by the lab and check on things,
and then I'm thinking about swinging through town and seeing
Spartan about some special plastic, if you know what I mean."

"Definitely, it sounds good to me. I got some business, too,
but I probably won't be getting up until after twelve. I'm getting the
feeling that I'm going to be a busy man in bed this morning." He
chuckled.

"That's cool. I'll see you when I get back."

They hung up. Ice headed downstairs and saw that Irene had
passed out on the sofa. He walked over, knelt down, and kissed her
on the cheek. She opened her eyes and smiled. She was as beautiful
as always.

"I'm going out for a little while. Deshea is a little stressed right
now. Try to talk to her for me, okay?"

She nodded. He walked into the garage and made sure that
everything was secure before he pulled out into the street.

The morning air was soft and breezy. He rolled down his window and allowed it to caress his face. Deshea entered his mind, and
he vowed that his unborn child would be raised to know the truth
about his father. He stopped at a red light.

"I kept my promise, Dad," he whispered.

The lab was being operated out of a trailer in a shabby park on
the south side of town. Ice walked in. The inside looked like something out of an old sci-fi movie: test tubes and large tanks filled with
boiling water were connected to sinks and other valves and gadgets.
Raul approached. He was dressed in a lab coat and a pair of green
goggles.

"How are you today, sir?" He extended his hand and they shook.

"Not bad. Irene gave me your message. What's the problem?"

Raul chuckled. "Oh, there is no problem, sir. We just need about two dozen more twelve-inch syringes. We have the others used up with Raw Ice, and they are frozen and incubating with extra ccs right now."

Ice held up his hand as if he had heard enough. "Look, Raul, forget the scientific bullshit terminology. Just say that you need money." He reached into his pocket and pulled out a small stack of hundred-dollar bills. "These Franklins should take care of everything." Raul took it and turned on his heel.

Ice walked over, picked up the phone, and dialed a number.

Deshea answered, "Hello?" Her voice sounded pleasant.

"Hey, baby, how are you feeling?"

"I'm okay. May Ling and Shortman are here, and we have a card game going on."

"I can dig it. But listen, I know things have been a little tense lately, so I was wondering if you would like to attend the Tyson-Seldon fight in Vegas tonight. The private jet is gassed up and ready to go."

She smiled. "I would love to, baby. You know how much I miss staying at the mansion out there, but I did promise May Ling that I would go with her to see a movie."

"Well, I will get four tickets, and we all can go. I'm sure she would enjoy seeing the Tyson fight, then watch a chick flick." He laughed.

"Okay, I will talk it over with them."

"Cool. Be dressed by 6:00 p.m. I'll see you then."

"Not so fast, mister. Aren't you forgetting something?"

He chuckled. "I love you."

"And I love you back." They hung up.

"Raul, give me a call tomorrow," he yelled.

Then he left. Once in the car, he pulled his delivery logbook from the glove compartment and studied the numbers carefully. It showed that six shipments of Raw Ice had been delivered to the streets over the last month. He started the car and pulled back onto the road. It was only a five-minute drive to Falcon's apartment in the center-city high-rise. He parked, grabbed his delivery book off the seat, and headed into the building. The doorman tipped his hat as he passed. He got onto the elevator and pushed the button for the nineteenth floor.

Something is wrong with the books. I know Falcon has a good answer for this, he thought to himself.

He stepped off the elevator and could hear the muffled sound of music as he approached the door. He rang the bell and the door was almost instantly answered by Falcon. "What's up, boss? I wasn't planning on seeing you today."

Ice smiled and stepped into the room. A naked woman and Jon, Falcon's roommate, were rolling around on the floor.

"It looks like you boys have your own circus going on here." Jon looked up and laughed.

"Do you wanna join us?" the woman asked.

"No, thanks, baby. I'm on a pussy-free diet. I'm watching what I eat." He took a seat on the couch and watched Falcon walk over to the radio and turn it down.

"So what's on your mind, boss?"

"I was just stopping in to review the books for the month."

Falcon looked at Jon. "Where did you put the logbook for the month?"

Jon got to his feet and headed down the hall. The woman wrapped herself in a blanket and sat on the love seat. When Jon returned, he was carrying a book; he handed it to Ice. Ice opened both and compared the numbers carefully. Falcon's book reflected that only four deliveries had been made, but Ice's book showed six.

Suddenly the uncontrollable demon of anger entered his body. He pulled out his smoke pole.

"Now, which one of y'all crackpots is Judas?"

He got to his feet. Jon looked over at Falcon, confused, then back at Ice.

"I'm Jon, boss. My name is not Judas. Who is Judas anyway?"

Falcon looked at his roommate. "Shut the fuck up, dumb ass. It's a Bible character who betrayed Jesus."

Ice cocked his weapon. "Someone better start singing soon because I'm getting a little impatient."

"Boss, I told Jon not to try it, but he wouldn't listen."

"Shut up, Falcon, you lying black bitch! You did that shit and you know it!" Jon snapped.

Ice laughed, "Y'all some real funny motherfuckers, especially you, Falcon. I trusted you with more than almost anyone."

"Boss, I'm sorry. It ain't what it appears to be." Ice laughed again.

"What it appears to be is one big fuck fest, and I'm the only one getting stuck with no Vaseline, might I add. But I like to fuck as well, so since you enjoyed fucking me, I'm going to fuck you. Now get naked, you slimy bastard." He aimed the gun at Falcon.

"Please, boss. Just give me another chance to make it right."

"I said get the fuck naked!" he snapped.

Falcon moved with lightning speed, and before you knew it, he was down to his boxer shorts. Ice looked over at the girl, who looked terrified.

"Have you ever seen this piece of shit naked?" She shook her head, indicating no. Ice turned his attention back to Falcon. "All right, off with the Calvin Kleins." He gestured with his weapon. Falcon trembled as he removed his last item of clothing. "Now get on all fours like the dog that you are." Falcon obeyed as beads of sweat ran down his face. Ice walked over and knelt behind him, then made eye contact with Jon. "This is what happens to motherfuckers who cheat and steal." He aimed the barrel inches away from his asshole. "Tell me if this is good sex," he said, pulling the trigger. The impact of the bullet knocked blood and guts from his mouth and took some of his teeth with it. He collapsed into death's arms instantly. The murder scene sent Jon into a frenzy. He jumped to his feet and ran nonstop toward the balcony, crashed through the glass window, and fell to his death. Ice walked over and looked. Jon's body was twisted, disfigured, as he lay lifeless on top of a parked car. He walked back into the room and looked at the trembling woman. "If you couldn't identify me, then I would let you live. I'm sorry, dollface." He picked up a pillow and covered her face, then pulled the trigger, knocking off one side of her once beautiful face. He had become possessed by his father's demon: a coldhearted, stoic, and diabolical creature sent from hell.

CHAPTER 2

"SO WHO DO YOU THINK is going to win the fight?" asked Ice, looking in the rearview as they pulled into the parking garage.

"I say Irion Mike in one."

"I don't think I can agree with that. The boy Seldon has one hell of a jab."

"A lot of dudes have good jabs, but Tyson's 'bout game, is all pro."

"Put your money where your mouth is, Shorty."

"Why is it that men have to always compete with one another?" Deshea interrupted.

"I guess it's the whole tough guy image," added May Ling.

Ice laughed. "Why is it that women are so nosy? If you see two people in the middle of the street arguing, nine times out of ten, you find an old lady nearby peeking out of her window." Everyone laughed. They parked, got onto the elevator, and made their way down to the street level of the MGM Grand.

People and street vendors were everywhere. A man with a shirt that read "Tyson vs Seldon" on it approached. "I got them hot Tyson T-shirts for sale," he said.

Ice looked at Deshea. "Do you want a shirt?"

She turned her lip upward. "I guess having a souvenir can't hurt."

He looked back at the vendor. "How much for two of them?"

"Twenty dollars a shirt," he responded.

Ice pulled out a crisp one-hundred-dollar bill and handed it to him. "Keep the change, and if you ever want a real job, look me up at Gaddafi's Palace in LA." He took the shirts and the four of them headed into the casino.

It was even more crowded, and you could see that most of the support was for Iron Mike. Suddenly a man passing shoved Ice aggressively. He turned and met eyes with Yana Kenichi, the son of Jakarta. They glared at one another briefly, then Yana gave a devilish grin.

"Babe, look!" Deshea tugged on his blazer excitedly. He turned around. "Ain't that Tupac and Suge Knight over there?" She pointed at the two men standing and talking with fans.

"Yeah, that's them," Shortman answered.

Ice chuckled. "I'm so used to seeing celebrities that it doesn't even surprise me anymore. Shit, every morning that I look in the mirror, I see a star." They all laughed. Ice turned and looked in the direction of where he saw Yana, but he had vanished.

The main event was short. Tyson flushed Seldon down the toilet like used Charmin.

"I told you that boy wasn't going to last against Mike." Shortman laughed as they exited the arena.

"You ain't got to rub it in, man. You won fair and square."

Deshea grabbed ahold of his arm. "Honey, I feel like I'm going to be sick."

He pulled her away from the chaos and caressed her face. "What's wrong, honey?"

"I don't know. I just feel light-headed, that's all."

"Go and get the car, Shorty." Ice tossed him the keys. He exited the door to the parking garage with May Ling. "Come on, let's rest your legs." He led her to a sofa near the exit.

"Do you think that Deshea is going to be all right?" May Ling asked.

"Yeah, it's just her pregnancy." They stepped from the elevator.

Suddenly the loud engine of a motorcycle could be heard. Shortman looked up and saw that the bike was approaching at high speed, and the figure on it was holding a large Samurai sword. He pushed May Ling to the ground, drew his weapon, and pulled the trigger twice. The realization that his gun had been emptied hit him all at once, but it was too late. He looked over at May Ling.

"I'm sorry," she whispered. The razor-sharp blade removed his head from his shoulders. His body took a second to collapse. May Ling let out a scream as the head rolled near her feet.

The motorcycle disappeared, then out from the shadows stepped Jakarta. He stood over May Ling, who was now kneeling next to Shortman's headless body. She looked up at him.

"I gave you what you wanted. Now leave!" she screamed.

Jakarta pulled out a weapon with a silencer connected. "You've disgraced your race and the honor of your family." He shot her twice in the chest and left her lifeless.

Deshea got to her feet. "I think I feel good enough to walk now. All this noise is giving me a headache."

"Are you sure, baby?"

"Yes, I'm ready to go." She gripped his hand tightly. As they stepped off the elevator, several police vehicles passed them. "I wonder what happened." She looked at Ice.

"I don't know. They are probably just chasing some kids in a stolen car or something." As they turned the corner, there was a crowd of onlookers, and police and forensic vans were everywhere. "Wait here," he said to Deshea and began to make his way through the crowd. Wicked thoughts entered his mind, and he hoped that they were selling him a false nightmare.

An officer stepped in his path. "Are you a friend or family to the deceased?"

Ice looked over his shoulder and could see Shortman's gator shoes, which were not covered from the sheet. Reality dropped the gavel on his heart.

"No, I'm not."

He turned and walked over to Deshea, who had made her way through the crowd and was standing nearby with tears streaming down her face.

"I thought you said everything would be okay."

He looked around to make sure that no one else had heard her outburst. "Baby, not here. Just trust me. I'm not going to let you get hurt."

"Trust you? Trust you? How can you say those words to me? Why don't you just give those people whatever they want so we can have a fucking family."

He pulled her farther from the crowd. "Look, Deshea, this thing is deeper than you can imagine. You're asking me to throw away everything that my father worked for. Something that was a part of me before there was a you."

"Do you mean to tell me that you're willing to die for this shit? I'm carrying your fucking child. What kind of life would it have without a father?"

"Look, Deshea, I promised my father that I'd live his dream."

She slapped him across the face. "Wake up! Do you even know the difference between dreams and nightmares?" He looked at her without giving a response. "Go to hell, Aldolphus Jackson!" She turned on her heel, walked over, and got back onto the elevator.

He walked past the crime scene down to his car, grabbed the spare key from under the wheel well, then drove into the Vegas night. He had lost one of his best friends, but he vowed that before this war was over, his death would be avenged. He pulled into the garage of his Vegas property, then gripped his smoke pole tightly before getting out of the vehicle. He entered the house. Tank and Irene sat wearing solid masks of gloom on their faces. He paused in the doorway; his smoke pole gripped tightly in his palm.

"I guess you guys have heard the news already."

Irene looked up at him. "Yeah, Deshea called. The poor girl is shattered. She said she is going back to her mother's." She paused. "I know you don't want to hear this, but whatever these people want from you, you should strongly think about giving it."

"I'm strongly going to give out hollow tips and closed caskets. This war is bigger than some damn formula. It's personal, real fucking personal. They took some of ours, and now I'm going to exterminate his whole fucking family."

Irene got to her feet and hugged him closely. "I will never betray you," she whispered, then left the room.

He looked over at Tank. "Are you my friend, Tank?"

His childhood friend stood up. "When we were kids, we made a pact: we are in this thing together, Aldolphus, until God finds a way for a true soldier."

Ice walked into his room and took a seat on the bed, then glanced over at the flashing light on the answering machine. He got to his feet, walked over, and pushed the button.

"Hello, Iceman, I'm sorry you missed our opening performance. No need to worry because there is more to see. You have exactly three hours from the time you hear this message to meet my demands. Oh, I forgot to tell you: you're already too late. Ha ha ha."

A black limo pulled in the front of a shabby apartment building. Jakarta put down the window and exhaled a cloud of cigar smoke into the air, then looked at his two loyal sons, Yana and Vay.

"Find out if he knows the formula before you kill him. If he knows it, bring him to me first."

"Yes, Father," responded Yana, grabbing a black bag from the seat and getting out of the vehicle.

They walked into the building, then up to the door of apartment B and knocked gently. A few seconds passed before they could hear the footsteps from the other side.

"Who is it?"

Yana cleared his throat. "We are here with a message from Ice." Vay smiled as they heard the locks.

Spartan opened the door and immediately turned as white as a ghost at the sight of the two men. He knew that they weren't Jehovah's Witnesses that had come to tell him about the latest *Watchtower* magazine. Before he could shut the door, Vay gave him a vicious thrust kick that knocked him backward into the apartment and onto the floor. They stepped inside and closed the door behind.

"Now you know what we want. You can either make it easy and tell us or die with the secret." Vay's tone was serious as he looked down on the near breathless Spartan.

"I don't know what you're talking about, and if I did, I wouldn't tell you fuckboys anyway. You might as well kill me dead."

Vay kicked him ruthlessly in the head. "Maybe that will give you some memory." Yana laughed.

"Rot in hell, you Japanese bastard."

They looked at one another and laughed. "Okay, you American piece of shit, you wanna play hard ball?"

Vay grabbed Spartan by the hair, then used an open palm strike to his forehead to render him temporarily unconscious. Yana opened his carry-along black bag and pulled a hammer and chisel from its contents.

"Hold his arms down," Yana said to his brother.

He placed the chisel onto Spartan's right palm and with one vicious swing of the hammer, pierced his skin and the hardwood floor. He let out a scream of agony as his hand was nailed to the floor. Yana walked to the other side of his body, where Vay was holding down his squirming arm. "Did you say that you're ready to talk?"

Spartan looked him in the eye. "Fuck you." He spat into Yana's face.

He laughed and wiped his brow, then placed another chisel onto Spartan's other hand and struck it even harder than the last time. His screams sounded like death posted around the corner of a murder scene. Vay straddled him and pinched his nostrils together so that his mouth would open, then Yana handed him a can of liquid Drano.

"I'm going to teach you about making racist slurs," he said as he poured the liquid into his mouth. You could hear it cooking like smoked meat on a grill. Spartan gargled blood and foam and squirmed for a moment until he collapsed into the arms of the man in the black cape.

It was in the early morning hours when Ice and his small army of soldiers stepped from the private jet and got into a waiting SUV. Kaila had called with some information about some restaurants that were owned by Jakarta. Ice deemed the info airtight and decided to make a house call, but he had to stop by and visit with Spartan about some Semtex bombs.

"Is everyone ready to take this war to these chumps?" He looked at Tank.

He laughed and opened his coat, displaying the two Uzis. "Let's kick some ass, baby boy."

Rock and Buddy were above words as they loaded assault rifles that were hidden under their long overcoats. The tension in the air could be cut with a knife, allowing each man to sink into a pool of the unknown.

This game had gone too far, but Ice realized that he was in too deep to run and hide. His friends and unborn child were depending on him to crush his adversaries and escape to the fog.

He parked in front of Spartan's building. "This is where the fun starts." He laughed as the four men left the vehicle. As they approached the apartment, Ice noticed that the door was slightly ajar. He pushed it open slowly. The sight of the dead body caused them all to pull their weapons and enter the room in a hysterical frenzy. Buddy, Tank, and Rock searched the residence while Ice knelt next to Spartan's gruesome remains. There was a note attached to his shirt. Ice picked it up and read the words. "You're late again, Mr. Iceman. We are getting close." Ice crumpled the paper and tossed it, then got to his feet. "Let's get the fuck out of here, boys. It's time for revenge."

Back in the car, he felt the fires of anger running through his veins. He looked at Tank. "Let's even the fucking score," he said through clenched teeth. He was determined to avenge the deaths of his slaughtered friends and more than willing to die for street justice. He had learned to play by his father's rules, the ruthless way, the way of the heartless trigger.

They parked across the street from Chow's Dragon-Styled Food. Ice looked at his companions.

"Let's do this."

They exited the vehicle and walked into the restaurant where a man dressed in chef's clothing stepped in their path.

"No Americans allowed." His accent was heavy.

Ice looked at Tank then back at the man. "I'm looking for Jakarta. Maybe you can tell me where to find him."

The man turned on his heel and walked through a set of double doors in the rear of the building. Tank looked at his best friend.

"I have a bad feeling about this one, Ice."

Suddenly, four armed men emerged from the rear doors and began firing reckless shots. Then several more shooters appeared. Tank let out a Rambo yell as he squeezed the triggers on his twin Uzis. Ice fired several shots and dropped a few bodies before he felt a burning sensation in his shoulder. He turned over a table and took cover, as he had felt the heat of several bullets miss his head by inches. He examined his shoulder and realized that he had been hit. His three companions continued to shoot and took cover when needed. The miniwar continued; then suddenly the gunfire ceased. The room was full of smoke, like someone had set off a bomb. Ice looked over at Buddy, who was stretched out on the floor behind a table with a large gaping hole in his leg.

"Who else is hit?" He looked at Tank, who was loading fresh clips.

"I'm good, baby boy."

Rock crawled over to Buddy. "We gonna get you out of here."

He picked him up from the floor. Ice and Tank got to their feet. Suddenly several more shots were fired; all hitting Buddy and instantly taking his life. Ice whirled around and let off five shots, striking the man who had appeared out of nowhere and dropping him to his death. Rock knelt next to his friend. Tank walked over and touched his shoulder.

"Come on, man. We can't carry no deadweight. No time to be a pallbearer." The trio left the bloody murder scene and escaped through the street fog.

Deshea walked into the living room and took a seat on the couch next to her mother, who was occupied with knitting a sweater. She hung her head in her palms.

"Girl, you need to get up off your tail and go back to that man."

"It's not that easy, Mama. I'm afraid of losing him to the streets."

"Take it from your mother: when your daddy was a young stud, he played those streets like a flexible part-time job, clocking in and out at different times, but it never stopped him from loving me. He was always home at night. You need to grab that man up before it's too late."

"Mama, I do love him, but I figured that the longer I stay away, the sooner he will realize the importance of us sharing a life together."

The older woman exhaled. "I only can give you advice, child. Eva didn't raise no stupid children, and neither did her daughter Marybeth. Sometimes experience is the best teacher."

The phone began to ring. Deshea got to her feet, walked to the kitchen, and picked it up.

"Hello?"

"Hey, baby, it's me. Can we talk?"

She slammed the receiver down, then walked back over and flopped down next to her mother. She ran her fingers through her hair in frustration. Her mother peered at her over the rim of her glasses.

"That was him again, I take it." Her voice was comforting.

A tear escaped Deshea's eye. "Mama, I just don't know what to do."

Her mother put down the sweater, wrapped her arms around her baby like she was a newborn, and allowed her to feel the pains of being in love.

"You're lucky that bullet went straight through." Irene added the last piece of tape to the bandage on Ice's shoulder.

"Thanks, Nurse." He laughed.

"Your nurse is that pretty little thang named Deshea. I'm just your aunt." She smiled.

"Why do you think she keeps hanging up on me?"

Irene sighed. "The girl is afraid, Ice. She loves you more than you can imagine. She will come around. You just got to give her a little time."

"I know this might sound crazy, but I feel stronger about her than I ever have about anyone."

She smiled. "It's only natural. She's pregnant with your child."

Tank entered the room. "You all right, soldier?"

Ice looked up at his friend and smiled. "I ain't dead yet, so I can't complain."

"I have the twins on the phone. Do you want me to give them any instructions?"

He thought for a moment. "Tell them to shut everything down and dispose of the product using the buckets of acid. Wire them each forty grand and tell them to leave town and lie low until I stomp out this fire."

"Anything else?"

"No, that's it for now. Thanks, Tank."

He left the room. Ice looked over at Irene.

"I wonder what Daddy would say if he could see me now."

She leaned over and kissed his cheek. "He would be proud of you. Just like me. You've grown to be a strong man just like your father." She got to her feet.

Ice reached out and grabbed her hand. "I love you," he said gently.

She leaned and kissed his forehead. "I love you too. End this war as quickly as possible. You have a family that needs you more than the battlefield does." He watched as she left the room.

Today he had come face-to-face with death, but for some reason, he didn't feel afraid. He almost embraced the feeling of standing in the fires of hell and looking Satan dead in the eye.

Jakarta slammed his fist down onto the table. "You mean to tell me that four men wiped out a whole army of trained killers?" He glared at the man before him.

Yana and Vay stood in silence at their father's side. "They had us outgunned, Uncle. We didn't realize that they were armed until the shots began to fly. I barely escaped with my life!"

Jakarta got to his feet, walked around his desk, and stood face-to-face with his trembling nephew. "You're a disgrace to this family!" he yelled.

"I know, Uncle. I have let you down."

"So you understand the recompense due to your error?"

"I do, Uncle, I do." He knelt before Jakarta and bowed his head.

Jakarta looked at Yana and nodded. He stepped from behind the desk and pulled his sword from its sheath and stood directly in front of his blood relative, then in one motion, he brought it down in the middle of his head with so much force that it split in half, killing him instantly.

Ice parked his car in the front of Deshea's mother's house. He walked up to the door and rang the bell twice. A black Jeep with tinted windows pulled along the curb and sat there momentarily, as if the vehicle had eyes of its own. He reached for his weapon, but without warning, the Jeep pulled back onto the street and disappeared.

"What are you doing here? Trying to get us killed?" He turned and saw Deshea looking out of an upstairs window.

"Deshea, can you just come down so we can talk?"

"Talk? Talk about what? Talk about how much money you make in a week or how many people you kill in a day?"

He sighed. "Look, Deshea, I don't understand why you're doing all this. You knew what I stood for when we first met. I realize that things have gotten a little out of hand. That's why I want to send you and your mama out of the country until this whole thing is over."

She chuckled. "You actually believe that I will leave the country behind your dumb shit? I don't think so, Aldolphus Jackson."

"Look, Deshea, it's not my fault that all this is happening. I didn't start this war, but I'm damn sure determined to end it."

"If it's not your fault, then whose is it? You're the one hiding shit from people. People who obviously don't give a fuck about you or what you stand for."

He shook his head in disgust. "I would rather die like a man than live like a coward." He turned on his heel and walked in the direction of his black Jaguar.

"I hate you Aldolphus Jackson. You hear me, you sorry motherfucker!"

He put down his window. "Let me give you a history lesson: you need to check the origins of the word *motherfucker*. I might be a lot of things, but that I am not." He put his window back up, then pulled out into the street.

Seasons change and people change, but here in the fast lane was a street romance going sour because the love of money and power had rained down and crushed their small planet.

The black limo parked in front of the shabby trailer. Jakarta took a long drag from his cigar, then looked at his two sons.

"You know what to do."

The two men exited the car and headed toward the trailer. Raul was closing the last box with duct tape when he heard the trailer door opening. He looked at Raffon.

"I'll be back." He walked out of the room and down the hall and was met by the two Kenichi brothers. He tried to speak, but the words were caught in a cocoon of fear, as Yana raised his Glock 17 with the silencer and pulled the trigger twice.

The first bullet struck him high in the chest, knocking him backward, and the second caught him directly between the eyes and left him lifeless. The two men walked down the hall and into the back room. Raffon looked up as they entered and knew that death had come to claim his soul. He closed his eyes as he was shot twice in the face, leaving an open, blooded mask.

Ice was walking into the house as the phone began to ring. He rushed over and picked up the receiver.

"Hello."

"Well done, Mr. Iceman. I was rather impressed with your little restaurant performance, but not enough to make me back off. I plan on seeing everyone inside of caskets." He laughed.

"Let me explain something to you, Mr. Jakarta: this war can go on forever, and you still won't get what you're after, so if you're willing to sacrifice your whole damn family over a lousy formula, then I have enough bullets to give away on your daughter's wedding day."

Jakarta laughed at his diatribe. "I admire your courage, Mr. Iceman, not bad for an upstart cowboy. But let this be your final warning: your chemists are dead, and next will be your pregnant girlfriend." The line went dead.

Ice wondered how Jakarta had so much information on him. "Money is power," he concluded. If death was the only way out, then he was prepared to take the ride for the survival of his family.

As usual, the casino was in full swing. The only difference on this night was that Tank, Ice, and the rest of the squad were seated in the back office, plotting their next method of attack on the bloody chessboard.

"I say we take our chances: go to the Jakarta Towers and bring the war to his front door. He's sure to be there." Tank finished, looking at Ice.

"That sounds like a suicide mission. We don't have enough soldiers for that. It's like going to a gunfight with a knife. What do you think, Rock?"

He looked at the six-foot-nine-inch bald man. Rock shifted his weight. "I agree with you, boss, but I also believe that the best strategy would be to continue to hit his restaurants and hope that we can flush him out that way. My mama always told me that the best way to bring a bear out of the woods is to fuck with its babies."

Ice chuckled then ran his fingers through his hair. "I wish Spartan was here because I would for sure blow those damn towers sky-high."

There was a knock at the door, and Kaila entered, carrying a white envelope. "This was in your mailbox." She handed it to Ice, and he studied it carefully.

"What is it, Ice?" Tank asked curiously.

"I don't know, but there's only one way to find out." He ripped it open and pulled out a piece of paper and began reading.

> I know you're in need of help. I realize that you are at war with the Kenichi mafia. So far, he has been one step ahead of you, but I have a bit of information that may prove useful. Tomorrow at 9:00 a.m., a mourning ceremony will be held at the Japanese Quonset for some of the family killed at the restaurant shooting. Yana and Vay Kenichi are expected to attend. It would be in your best interest to make an appearance. I will be in touch to inform you of any new developments.
>
> A friend,
> LACW

Ice folded the paper and looked around at his crew. "It looks like someone is on our side in all this," said Tank nonchalantly.

"The idea is good, but I think Jakarta is behind it."

"I have to disagree, man. If Jakarta was behind this, do you think he would tell us where to find them? And not only that. How many gangsters other than us will show up to a funeral strapped?"

"You have a good point, Tank, but I still feel a little uneasy about a mystery inside helper that goes by LACW. That shit just smells funny to me."

"Look, man, we gotta start taking some chances out here. If we don't, them motherfuckers will bury all of us in a New York minute, and I ain't ready to check out of this hotel just yet. So I say we take it to them just like we did at the restaurant."

There was a long silence as Ice allowed his friend's words to sink into his confused and undecided mind. He got to his feet. "Okay, here's the plan: we go over to the Quonset tonight and install cameras. That way we know that it's not a setup. Then we wait in the van until the mice run onto the sticky trap and close the curtains." He paused. "Rock, you and Monster grab some of the old cameras and monitors out of the security office. Nutso, you and Moose grab up four more men. Tank, you bring around the van. And I want everyone ready to move in twenty minutes." He turned and walked away.

As he entered the dice table room, Irene approached.

"What's going on?"

"Nothing. I just need for you to leave here before long. Go home and lock everything up. I will have people outside of the doors, so no need to worry. And don't answer the phone unless you hear my voice on the machine."

"Aldolphus, please tell me what's going on!"

"Just do what I said!" he snapped then walked away.

She stood, watching him walk away; he reminded her so much of Airstead, and God only knew how much she was afraid of losing him. But she realized that he was a man, now ruthless and stoic like his father. Her only hope was that he would make it to see thirty.

After installing the cameras in the Japanese Quonset, the early morning hours seemed to arrive at light speed. Ice and his crew watched the monitors patiently from the van as the parking lot began to see its first signs of activity. Tank looked at Ice.

"It looks like our little tip payed off." He smiled as a black limo pulled up and parked.

"Looks like you're right, Tank."

"I told you that some chances are good ones." They studied the monitors closely.

"Jackpot. Look at who just arrived." You could hear the excitement in Ice's voice. Yana and Vay got out of a limo and entered the building.

"Where in the hell is Jakarta?" questioned Tank.

"I don't know, but we have to take whatever fish that bites. Can you dig it? If we don't catch the big one, then I'm cool with the appetizer."

They watched the monitor more closely as everyone in attendance removed their shoes and knelt to the floor, facing the several urns that had been placed on some sort of altar. They chanted and clapped their hands in sequence. Tank looked at Ice.

"What kind of a funeral is that?" He chuckled.

"I don't know. I'm not into the salvation business. I'm all about retribution. Now let's go and get some."

They began to load their weapons; each man immersed in his own thoughts. Ice felt that today; this gangland war would bury itself in an ancient cemetery. Yesterday's story was a story that could only be told by the survivors themselves. Ice pulled out a bag of blue powder and snorted some before passing it around to the other six men on this mission for vengeance.

"Let's make the news, boys."

He opened the sliding door of the van, and each man exited like a trained soldier. Tank led three shooters to the back entrance, while Rock and JJ went to the front. Ice made his way through the parking lot and up to the tinted window of the black limo that he saw Jakarta's sons get out of. He tapped on it gently, and it rolled down instantly.

"Are you the driver for the Kenichi family?"

"No English, sir," the driver responded.

Ice pulled the mini tech from his coat and pointed it in his face. "How about now? Do you understand this dialect?"

He pulled the trigger twice, and the driver slumped over in the seat; a soft mist could be seen coming from the two holes in his chest. Ice pushed his lifeless body over into the passenger seat and put on the newsboy cap that he had been wearing. JJ looked at Rock, then took a deep breath before opening the doors.

"Burn in hell!" he yelled as he and Rock tossed the smoke bombs into the room. The rear doors flew open and in came Tank and his shooters.

"It's party time, motherfuckers!"

They ran down the aisles, cutting down any and every person moving. The rapid gunfire mixed with blood-gurgling screams were horrifying. The cries of innocence were just mere echoes in a battle-field. Yana and Vay managed to escape out of a side window, ran to the limo, jumped into the back seat, and began hammering on the dividing window.

"Get us out of here now!" Ice started the vehicle, then put down the power window. He looked them both in the eye and swore that he could see Shortman's reflection. "It's Retribution Day. You fucks have lost your salvation." He pulled the trigger several times, each bullet hitting vital spots like names had been written on the backs of them. I guess bullets do have names.

The war was finished, and Ice and his goons were taking home the victory.

They drove in silence until they reached the house. Ice looked at his comrades.

"Tonight, we celebrate our victory: I want everyone at the casino by 9:00 p.m. I'm paying for everything." He got out of the van.

"Hey, Ice, tell Kaila I will see her later tonight. It's nothing like a good shot of pussy after a hard day at work." Tank laughed.

"I told you to leave that girl alone before you end up strung out like that Uncle Tom Orenthal James." The gang laughed at Ice's humor.

"Shit, bro, ain't no pussy good enough to kill for." Tank slid over into the driver's seat and started the van.

Irene and Kaila were seated on the couch when Ice walked in. "It's all over now," he blurted.

Irene looked at him curiously. "What do you mean it's all over?"

"The war between the Kenichi family and us. We took out the heart of his camp."

Irene sighed. "You can take heart all you want, baby boy, but if you don't have Medusa's head in hand, then the war is just getting started."

"Listen, Auntie, I don't think Jakarta is stupid enough to keep fighting a war that he clearly can't win."

"I don't believe that you're thinking clearly, Ice. Jakarta is a wicked and diabolical human. As soon as we relax, then he is bound to kick up some more dust. I think we should all leave town for a few months until everything settles."

"There is no way that I will run from a coward like Jakarta. He is nothing without his sons, and they are both in court with God at the moment, trying to plead a case for salvation." He laughed.

"I'm not asking you to run away. I just think that a lot of us are in more danger than you choose to acknowledge. That's the difference between you and Airstead: when he took care of a problem, he made sure that it was done correctly, with no loose ends at all."

Anger rushed through his veins. "Fuck you! You lowlife bitch! My father made you into who you are today. If you wanna leave, then go. I guess I was wrong about you: ain't you the same woman who told me that I had to be a soldier to live my father's dream, or was that just the rum talking?"

Irene got to her feet and slapped him across the face. "Wake the fuck up out of that dream you're in before it turns into a nightmare. This isn't a game anymore, Aldolphus. Look around you, boy, and see who's missing. They want your secret, or all of us in graves." She stood akimbo. He rubbed his cheek where he had been struck.

"I'm going out for a bit, and when I return, I don't want to find you here." He turned and walked down the hall.

Irene stood wearing a mask of sorrow as she watched him disappear. He pulled onto the street, confusion a nonstop locomotive in his mind. How could a dream that was passed down to him turn so quickly into a gruesome nightmare, full of bloody shattered pieces? He suddenly made a U-turn and headed in the direction of Deshea's house. He would convince her and her mother to leave town at once. He was drowning in so many thoughts that the normally sharp Ice didn't even notice the black SUV that had been following close behind.

The white delivery van pulled up to the nice home on Hope Road. The driver put on his sunglasses and hat, then grabbed the two dozen roses from his companion on the passenger side.

"This shouldn't take long. Just keep an eye out."

He climbed from the vehicle. Deshea and her mother were seated in the living room watching a Ron O'Neal movie when the doorbell sounded.

"I will get it, hon. Just check on the hot dogs. They should be just about done boiling."

Her mother got up from her chair and headed over to the door, and Deshea headed down the hall to the kitchen.

"Who is it?"

"It's Julia's Flowers with a delivery."

The older woman smiled as she unlatched the door and opened it. She found herself looking into a little black hole. The goon squeezed the trigger of the silenced Magnum; the first bullet struck her in the neck, knocking her backward. The second one landed in her chest, and before her body hit the ground, another one struck her in the ear, knocking it off. He stepped into the house and dropped the roses next to her lifeless body.

"Who was it, Mama?" Deshea yelled from the kitchen. She wiped her hands, then turned to see a man with a high-caliber weapon standing in the doorway.

"Why don't you make this easy for me and come with us without a fight?" His voice was calm.

"Fuck you!"

She turned and grabbed the boiling pot of water from the stove and tossed it in his face. The skin on his bones bubbled and melted away like wax. He screamed in agony and ran toward her, gun still in hand. She took a step to the side and swung the empty pot, striking him in the head and knocking him to the floor. His body was still cooking as she ran past him.

"Help me! Please someone! Help me!"

She ran into the waiting arms of the other man. He quickly inserted a syringe containing a clear liquid into her neck, taking the fight out of her almost instantly as she sank into limbo.

The limo parked outside the large fortress. Jakarta looked at his four henchmen.

"Bring the aunt out alive. Anyone else, I want dead."

Kaila was asleep on the couch as Irene gathered some of her things from an upstairs bedroom, and that was when she heard a thud that sounded like it came from the balcony. She paused a moment before deciding that it was nothing. She zipped the bag shut and was headed out of the room when she heard a crashing noise coming from downstairs. Kaila jumped to her feet, but death had already approached. The goon grabbed a handful of her hair and used a straight razor to slit her throat. Next, he covered her head with a plastic bag and taped it. She fell to the floor and convulsed until her soul took flight. Irene raced down the stairs and found two large men standing in her path. The syringe entered her skin, and she went limp and fell to the floor.

An overwhelming feeling of fear overtook Ice as he pulled up to Deshea's mom's house. The block was filled with cop cars and ambulances. He jumped out of the vehicle and rushed through the small crowd of people that had gathered outside.

"Hold it, sir." An officer stepped in his path.

Ice's rage meter had already maxed out; he grabbed the officer up in the collar and forced him to the ground. Another officer jumped onto his back and attempted to put him in a choke hold. He flipped him, then lifted his body above his head and tossed him into the crowd of spectators.

"He's got a gun!" yelled a voice; and then he was swarmed by several officers with blackjacks. They looked like they enjoyed nothing better than inflicting bodily harm. They struck him several times before his body fell to rest against his strong will. He woke up on a concrete slab in the basement of the police station. He clutched his left side as pain shot through his stiff, battered body. Though the pain was great, he realized that he needed to get out of jail and soon. He slowly got to his feet and walked over to the mirror and examined himself closely.

"Not so pretty today," he whispered.

"Aldolphus Jackson."

He turned and saw a tall female officer standing outside his cell. He walked over.

"Look, I need to get out of here, not now, but right now."

She smirked. "Your bail has been paid, and your vehicle is parked outside of the station, but I have a few questions that I need to ask. How well did you know Marybeth Williams?"

"I know her. She is my girlfriend's mother."

She wrote on a small tablet. "You mean you did know her. She was found deceased at her home tonight."

He felt like he had been hit by a ton of bricks. He wanted to ask about Deshea but decided against it; he didn't want to involve Johnny Law no more than they already were.

"Can I ask why you were carrying a loaded firearm without a license?"

"I do have a license. Just not one to carry, but the reason is that I own Gaddafi's Palace, so I have to keep an insurance policy." He winked. She felt herself blush but dared to show it. After more questions, she opened his cell.

"Okay, you're free to go for now."

He walked past her and smiled, then turned on his heel.

"If you ever get tired of punching the clock for a living, then check me out. I might have a job for you. And yes, you can keep the uniform. It makes you look dominant." She blushed again; this time she couldn't hide it. He walked out into the parking lot and got behind the wheel of the car and pulled into the street.

Irene had been right when she said things had already gone too far, but hearing her say it only made it hurt more. He was a rich man but felt void of life's many treasures, alone and sheltered just like that lost child that he once was, living in the dark gloomy shadows called the ghetto.

He entered the house and noticed that it was in shambles. He pulled out his weapon and made his way into the living room and knelt near the couch where he saw a few drops of blood. He got to his feet and raced upstairs hoping to not find Irene splattered somewhere. The phone rang, and he picked it up in a hurry.

"Tank, tell me this is you," he said.

"Your time has expired, Iceman. You've murdered my only two sons, and now I will take away your future, unless of course you can produce the formula, and I might consider letting someone live, and this war can end for the both of us. You lack the common sense to make it in this game, kid."

"You fuckin' bastard. If anything happens to my family, you're going to die a slow and painful death."

Jakarta laughed. "Calm yourself. You are in no position to negotiate the terms of the treaty. Now, be at the White Sands Beach at 10:00 p.m. tonight, and make sure to come alone and keep the heroics in the back of your mind. I want that formula."

"Go to hell, you slanted-eye pig."

Jakarta laughed again. "I love your comedy, but what you have failed to realize is that you're already in hell, Mr. Iceman, and you're melting at a fast pace. Now I have one more key instruction, so listen up: leave your vehicle and take a taxi, and if you think about trying some funny stuff, then I left you a gift in the closet that might make you think again." The line went dead.

Ice looked over in the direction of the closet; his heart pounding as he approached. He noticed drops of blood outside the door as he reached out and snatched it open. The sight made him vomit instantly. Kaila had been cut into pieces and her head was placed on the shelf with a piece of paper sticking out of her mouth. He turned his head away from the scene and reached up and removed the note. His breathing was heavy, and his hands a constant tremble as he opened it. "Deshea and Irene are next. Choose the right decision." He crumpled the note and dropped it to the floor. *How could I've been so blind as to leave the two people that I love the most unprotected?* he thought to himself.

He walked over to the portrait of Airstead that hung on the wall and removed it, revealing a safe. He opened it and pulled out two handguns and the disk containing the formula. He walked down to the library and took a seat and momentarily thought about calling Tank and planning an ambush. But he quickly decided against it, realizing that any false move would bring him and his loved ones to embrace an early death. He dumped a large bag of the blue powder onto the desk and marveled at the small mountain before grabbing a playing card out of the desk and scooping up a large amount and snorting it up. He continued to consume the drug until his face and body were numb to pain or the fear of death. There was no escaping the vicious hand of fate; the world was a prison within itself, and any true thug knows that death is the only freedom for the captive soul.

He was standing alone, like a flower without water; a young man who would one day become a legend in his own time and talked about for generations after.

It was breezy and dark when the taxi dropped Ice onto the dirt road that led to the beach. He made his way through a short, wooded path, then stepped out onto the pure white sand. The dark clouds rushed by, guided by high-altitude winds. The blood moon cast a glow that radiated the secluded stretch of beach, which had been chosen as the meeting ground. Suddenly four bright headlights blinded him, causing him to raise a hand to his face. It took a moment for him to see the silhouette of a man standing a few feet away.

"Turn off the lights," he requested. The lights went off, leaving the blood moon the only light.

"I'm glad that you've accepted my invitation, Mr. Iceman. I almost thought that I would have the pleasure of giving your girl-friend a C-section." Jakarta laughed. "But I can see that she means something to you. Maybe you're not a coward after all. Now, show me the disk containing my formula."

Ice thought for a moment and wondered how Jakarta even knew that there was a disk. "Show me my family first."

Jakarta turned to the black Jeep. "Bring them out!" he yelled.

Ice looked on as the door opened: from a distance, he could make out a large man and two women. As they approached, the moonlight fell upon their faces, and Ice felt his heart hit the sand as he looked into the eyes of the large man who stood before him.

Never in a million years would he suspect this sort of betrayal. Life had a way of repeating the strong and crucial events of the past.

The revelation of deceit rained down on him as he thought back to the note that had tipped him off to where to find Jakarta's two sons. LACW aka Los Angeles Clyde Williams, also known as Tank, his best childhood friend.

"Tell me it isn't so. Tell me it wasn't you this whole time." He was almost pleading.

Tank smiled devilishly. "This is reality, Aldolphus, not some fucking movie script that you contrived in your mind."

"How could you do this after all that we've been through together? We are friends, Tank."

Tank chuckled. "It's called money and power, Aldolphus. Something that I've been striving for, for a very long time. And you're in the way."

Jakarta laughed before speaking. "Isn't it funny, Iceman, how businessmen share some of the same associates. The only difference between you and me is that I offer a better salary, but that's obvious."

Ice looked at Deshea and Irene, who were both gagged and tied to one another. He could read the words of fear in their eyes and felt as if the hourglass had truly run out.

"Tank, it's not too late to change your mind. We can work this out," he said as tears became strong behind his lids.

Ice was alone and realized that at this point, only one person would probably walk away alive. Tank smiled.

"You're right, Ice. I did change my mind."

He quickly pulled his weapon and took aim at Jakarta. Jakarta's eyes grew large in astonishment as Tank squeezed the trigger, and the heated bullets of betrayal approached Jakarta at light speed, hitting his forehead and knocking his brains out of the back of his skull. His body stood momentarily then collapsed to the sand.

Tank turned and glared at his best friend. "It's just you and me now, baby boy. Like the old days."

Ice let a tear fall from his eye. "This isn't the way it's supposed to end. What happened to 'One for all, back to back, until God finds a way for a true soldier?'" His words hung in the air like a hot-air balloon.

Tank shook his head. "Don't you get it, Aldolphus? This is God's plan. I'm tired of being spoon-fed by you. I can run my own damn organization, and the only way to do that is to eliminate the shining star, which is you, my friend."

"Tank, I loved you like a brother. You know damn well that what's mine is yours. We can walk away from this thing together. The way that it's supposed to be."

Tank laughed again. "I would be a fool to walk away with you knowing that at any time, you might shoot me in the back. I don't think so, Ice. I'm smarter than you give me credit for."

Ice took a deep breath. "Please, Tank, let my family go. This has nothing to do with them."

"I'm afraid I can't do that. Are you worried about your unborn child?" Tank reached over and rubbed Deshea's stomach. "No need to worry. I will take him under my wing just like he's one of my own."

Ice felt his frustration starting to build. "Tank, don't throw it all away over money and power. We can fix this."

"Shut up! I'm tired of hearing your fucking mouth!" he snapped. "Now, I'm going to give you a chance to go for your weapon because I know that you have it on you. You can either go out like Billy the Kid or die like Buckshot Willy."

Ice smirked at his humor. "If you let my family go, you can have anything that you want: a Wild West gunfight or a bare-knuckle brawl."

Tank thought for a moment; his face gloomy and dark as the moonlight caressed it. "I accept." He pulled out a knife and cut the rope that bound the women together. Then he removed the tape from their mouths. "Now don't either one of you bitches try any funny stuff." He pointed his gun at them, then reached out and grabbed a handful of Irene's hair.

"Please don't hurt me," she whimpered.

"Shut up, bitch!" He shoved her to the ground.

She quickly got to her feet, and out of fear and hysteria started running toward Ice. Deshea covered her face and sank to the ground. "Irene, don't! Please don't!" Ice screamed, but it was a late cry for mercy.

Tank lifted his gun and took aim.

"Good night, beautiful."

He fired two shots. The first hit her in the shoulder and exploded into her chest, but her will to survive was so strong that the hot bullet only slowed her momentarily. The second struck her spine. Her lifeless body collapsed into Ice's arms.

"Nooo!" His screams echoed off the crash of the water. He let Irene's limp body fall to the ground as he raised his weapon.

The clock read triple zeros, and this would be his last shot. It was as if everything was happening in slow motion. Both men took aim, and the war began. Bullet against bullet, friend against friend.

Deshea was only inches away as some of Tank's blood hit her shirt, and the big man fell hard to the sand like Goliath. She got to her feet and looked at Ice, who was still standing with gun in hand. She ran toward him. *It was finally over, and things would be different,* she thought.

Suddenly Ice collapsed to the ground. Deshea's nightmare had become a reality as she knelt next to his body and noticed two bleeding wounds in his chest. She lifted his head into her palms as tears streamed freely down her cheeks.

"Don't leave me like this, Ice. Please! We have so much to live for. So many things to see together!" she cried. He reached up with his blood-soaked hand and touched her stomach; then in a short flash, his dream of the small child relived itself.

He was standing alone in a large cemetery, the air was cold and wet as he walked, and the cries of a thousand owls entered his ears. Then he heard the voice, *Leave the people. You're alone. Fight alone and die alone. Leave the people before it's too late.*

The child approached. *Daddy, don't let the monster get me, please, Daddy,* he cried.

It had all been a revelation, a vision of some sort.

"I love you, Deshea." He forced a smile.

The cold entered his body, and then death closed the door of blackness on his soul.

ABOUT THE AUTHOR

PENNY WISE WAS BORN IN the nation's capital and raised in one of the toughest housing developments in the city, where he was exposed to the gritty underworld streets. Being one of nine children, his Mother did the best she could for the family. But after she was brutally murdered, an eleven year old Penny moved to Harrisburg PA, where his troubled life seemed to chase him. In and out of homes and facilities, including foster care, he was forced to survive the only way that he knew. Eventually he ended up homeless, and was raised by the streets for some time. He is now a small business owner and a proud father of a three year old boy whom he loves dearly.

CPSIA information can be obtained
at www.ICGtesting.com
Printed in the USA
BVHW031314190320
575452BV00001B/18